El Condor

Oew Sook Kim

El Condor

Translated by Bruno Yoon H Lee

The characters and events portrayed in this book are fictitious. Any similarity to real persons, living or dead, is coincidental and not intended by the author.

ISBN-13: 9798843454616

Cover design by: Mi Young Oh
Library of Congress Control Number: 2018675309
Printed in the United States of America

For my husband, Reverend James Hills, who adopted Anna and never had the chance to read my book due to the language difference.

Contents

El Condor

1. Tree House

Finally, the wind from Lake Ontario blew in, carrying the smell of rotten eggs with it. As the wind died down, the immigrant workers who spent the winter in their homelands, resumed their work in the vineyards.

Father inspected the tree house and the ladder that had suffered through the long cold. Our Father had built the tree house on top of the oak tree in our backyard, when Brian and I were young. The tree house is a treasure trove that keeps the memories of Brian and I chattering, laughing, reading books, playing the zamponya, Brian's unfamiliar voice as he grew out of his puberty, my bashful voice, and the ever so slightly improved sound of my zamponya. As soon as Father told me the ladder was safe to climb, I grabbed my zamponya and scurried up into the tree house. As I looked down onto Lake Ontario through the small window, the lake transformed into Lake Titicaca from my homeland, Peru, and shone underneath the blue sky.

I placed the instrument to my mouth, watching a flock of birds flying across the sky. Afraid of losing the fading memories like a breath exhaled, the zamponya is my way of clinging to the past. My Father tied the reeds together with Mother's hand woven five color strings. This instrument encompassed the touch of my parents and even my brother's breath.

I began to gently blow into the reed as if my brother, Mario, told me to follow him as he closed his eyes, softly placed the zamponya on his lower lip, and blew as if breathing life into the zamponya.

"O Almighty Condor, Lord of Heaven,
Take us to our home in the Andes."

The melody was El Condor Pasa. A song that my brother's lips seemed to play with and to weep and now a song that's familiar to my lips as well.

As I remembered the time when I was a six year old Mamani, in front of my eyes was Lake Titicaca where the water reeds began to dance to the gentle waves created by a flock of birds taking to the sky.

As my Father returned home from catching Turcha, the slow setting sun on the horizon behind my Father turned deep orange. Thanks to the orange sunset, Father's face was always the color of dirt. It was perhaps due to the sunburn from the harsh sunlight or it was just his, no, just the color of his people, Peruvians.

"O, Almighty Condor, wait for me at the main square of Cuzco in Inca.

Let us walk through Machu Picchu and Huayna Picchu."

"Ah, Anna!"

As my longing weeped along with the melody, a soft voice wrapped around my shoulders from behind, along with an arm. I was back as Anna from my six year old Mamani-self, but I didn't take the zamponya off my lips.

The arm squeezed my shoulders. Then he buried his face in the back of my neck.

I wanted that moment to last forever. His tightening arm, his face buried in the back of my neck, and his breath, I wanted to revel in his touch.

But I knew, we both needed to stop.

"Are you going to keep doing this to your sister, Brian?"

I left my shoulder where it was, acting like an older sister only in words.

I just couldn't bring myself to show him my burning desire to turn around and hug him.

It was right then. 'Plump!' A dull sound of something falling, followed by a groan from outside. 'Oww! Oww!'

In a fleeting moment, I threw my zamponya to the ground as Brian took back his arm and bounced outside. He was already climbing down the ladder.

"Mom!"

"Mother!"

Brian and I, not knowing what to do, just cried out for her. Mother had fallen on a patch of dry grass underneath the tree.

Around her were pieces of broken cookies, with the plate way over yonder.

"The cookies came out really well so..."

Mother tried to cover up her embarrassment with the cookies.

She must've fell when she climbed up through the door that Brian had quietly opened and forgot to close, and unexpectedly saw what we were doing.

"Brian, call 911. Hurry!"

"No! Don't! It wasn't that high."

I think Mother wanted to deny what she saw even with the embarrassment. As if to prove she was alright, Mother sat up and covered her exposed calves with her disheveled skirt.

Brian and I helped her lie down on her bed, and made some hot tea.

"Anna, you are my daughter. Brian's older sister."

Mother held onto my hands holding the cup of tea. I stood next to Mother and her low 'as a matter of fact' sound of her voice drew a piercing blood-red line across my heart, as she looked deep into my eyes. I couldn't look into her eyes.

"Yes, mother."

With my head down, it was the only answer that I could and should say. It was an answer that I had to force myself as the touch of his arm around my shoulder and his face buried in the back of my neck still lingered in my memory.

"What were you thinking, climbing the ladder? You thought you were still young!"

Father returned home from the winery, pale as a ghost, and joked. Not knowing what Mother saw, Father was glad Mother wasn't hurt and was adamant that she would never climb the ladder again and enjoy the cookies at home.

"You're right. I used to be a good climber, but I guess I'm old now."

Mother bitterly smiled.

I thought this would pass as it did. But Mother wanted to hear it from Brian as well.

After a few days of rest, Mother called Brian. I already knew what she was going to say to Brian. The same thing she said to me. It was a

feeling that we had for eachother even though we grew up as siblings.
"You are Anna's little brother, Brian!"
"I don't want to be anymore, Mom!"
As I prepared hot tea, the short but strong words from Mother and Brian's sharp voice knowing what Mother was thinking, clashed from the onset.
"Brian, you two started as brother and sister!"
"Why do you get to decide? Anna never said she wanted to be my older sister, did she?"
As Mother said one thing, Brian added several more. It was a rebellion I had never seen before. I felt my heart tightening.
Words no longer came out of Mother's mouth. It was obvious she couldn't speak from the shock.
I knew what Brian was feeling. We might've started as brother and sister, but that was no longer the case. It was what I wanted to say when Mother told me while holding my hand. 'Mother, I don't want to be Brian's older sister anymore.' But I wasn't like Brian, who could speak his mind whenever he wanted. Nobody forced me to, but I always kept quiet when I had something to say and I grew up that way because I always thought that's what I had to do. That was my limit.
"But it still doesn't make it right, Brian!"
After a moment of silence, Mother raised her voice again.
"That's why you think Mom!"
Brian cut her off like a sharp knife.
"Is this how you talk to your mother, Brian?"
I hurriedly came out of the kitchen. I understood how Brian felt, but still, a child shouldn't be so disrespectful to his mother. It was his fault for cornering Mother with his words. As much as I didn't want to, I had to be a daughter and a big sister in front of Mother. I needed to reassure her of me and Brian's relationship. That was the reason for my being.
"Anna!"
Brian looked at me dumbfounded as if he'd been hit upside the head. I took advantage of the moment.
"You're my younger brother, Brian!"
Brian gawked at me in silence, as I spoke firmly, hiding my longing to be one with him. I'll never forget Brian's face as he looked at me with a, 'How can you say that to me' look on his face.
But I had to keep my composure and be firm. It was because Brian's

words became disrespectful and forced, the moment they left his mouth. It was because his words were denying the fact that we were living with the promise of an accepted relationship.

Otherwise, there was no way to reassure Mother, to suppress Brian's feelings, and most importantly, to stop my burning desire for Brian. It was a cold, harsh reality, opposite from the long simmering feelings between Brian and I.

'This is it, Brian.'

I wanted to cry, as Brian just looked at me in silence. Surprised, Mother looked at me and Brian with her eyes wide open.

A few months later, Brian left the house with his big bag pack. He said he was going to a country unfamiliar to me. Korea. It was probably because of what I said. 'You're my younger brother, Brian.'

I couldn't catch him or leave with him. All I could do was watch. It was probably the same with our parents. They'd already buried the pain of losing their son deep in their hearts.

"I won't be long. Take care of our parents, Anna."

It was Brian's way of making sure I wouldn't take off too.

So Mother, Father, and I desperately waited for the son who would return home soon, without knowing when that day would be.

2. Calm Excitement

The news of Brian's homecoming stirred the house with a calming excitement. It was like a gentle surface of a lake, right after the spring breeze danced around. Father fixed up Brian's room, and Mother, as if nothing could be done around the house without me, called out, 'Anna, Anna', as scurried around the house. It was as if a crystal bell was tied around Mother's voice.

"You can tidy up their room, right Anna?"

When Mother asked to clean up the newlywed's room, I had to desperately hold back calling out to her. 'Mother!' In truth, Mother's words were just as soft and gentle as any that no one could refuse her.

But I'm sure it was her intention for me to wash away any leftover feelings for Brian, as I cleaned the newlywed's bedroom. Or maybe not. I could've been her way of saying to be not persuaded by any lingering feelings and to be strong as an older sister.

Mother's gentle request felt like the last remaining root of my tortured feeling was being cut away. Still, I had to place the bed and the dresser, put on new curtains, and make the bed with the bed cover that I made with Mother.

With the quilt cover neatly covering the new bed, I looked down at the quilt cover. It was something that Mother and I made when Brian and I were still in college. Mother said she'd give it to Brian someday when he got married.

I'm sure Mother was relieved that I was helping to clean the newly wed's room, then. She probably thought the long deep feelings that came about while growing up together had taken care of itself, as I cleaned my younger Brother's room.

However, as I cut the fabric and wove them together into geometric shapes, all I could think was, 'I want to cover up with Brian.' To sleep with Brian, to wake up with Brian, have Brian's child, with Brian, and with Brian...

I knew this was a forbidden desire, so I thought of the drawings in the plains of Nazca, Peru. The mythical drawings in the Nazca plains, located on the southern coast of Peru.

Although my Father, my brother, or anyone in the family had never been to Peru, if you didn't know about the drawings that our ancestors left, you weren't Peruvian. It was said that the Father of Peru was one of the drawings. The symbol of freedom and the immortal bird, Condor.

However, the pattern that Mother and I wove was not that of a bird, but a flower. A bloomed flower on the newly wed's bed.

There was a time I wished to be that flower. I would daydream that I became that flower and fell asleep next to Brian. I pretended to make a mistake and pierced my finger with the needle to comfort myself.

Was it because Brian was the first person I loved and no one else? Even though I understood why Mother was asking me to clean the newly wed's room, I was pained by her cruelty. Perhaps she asked me because she knew all too well of her daughter's feelings and she wanted to keep me in my place one more time.

By this time tomorrow, Brian will be returning home from Korea with his wife. As soon as Brian appears with his wife in front of Mother, all her worries will disappear as if there never were any. The mother and son relationship will continue as if nothing had happened. That was the promise made between adults a long time ago.

Back when I was young, not knowing what was said between my Peruvian Father and Brian's family; and even if I did know, I wasn't old enough to express my thoughts so I just had to go along as the adults said. Amongst the discussion between the adults, my older brother Mario became angry at our father and cried over and over again. A year passed after we first met and as I followed Brian's family to Canada, the only person that changed in my young eyes was my older brother, Mario.

Mario played the zamponya as he cried and drank chicha just like our father. Then he became rough.

'Are you going to be responsible for Mamani, Mario?'

'I'll take care of Mamani, Dad!'

Whenever our Father said something, my brother stood against him. My gentle older brother Mario became increasingly rough, then started using violence, drunk from the chicha. It was as if he became another person.

'The Hills family says they'll raise our Mamani as their daughter.'

'Wherever Mamani goes, you or I won't be there!'

Even though our father reassured Mario with Brian's family's promise, Mario did not understand.

'If your mother was with us, I wouldn't do this Mario. Without Manami, I too...'

Father also drank the chicha and my brother became more violent.

Through the promise of adults, I, who was once called Mamani, became the daughter of the Hills family and grew up as Anna Hills. As Brian's older sister.

Looking down at the bed, I finally grabbed a pruning shear and walked out to the garden in the yard. The garden was something that Mother and I took care of together.

I knelt down in front of a patch of dark purplish chrysanthemums that had yet to wither. I grabbed the ends and cut a basket of the flowers. The scent vibrated through the air.

Scent that would fill the newlywed's bedroom.

3. The Harsh Reunion

Brian called several days ago, politely declining Father's offer to pick him at the airport, saying that he'll take the airport limousine.

'Do you think he's still bitter?'

Mother was planning to meet her son and daughter-in-law at the airport, but she was disappointed at Brian's words. I'm sure she was thinking back to when Brian left for Korea three years ago.

'What, upset? He's just telling us not to drive all the way out there.'

Knowing what Mather meant, Father turned the conversation to driving. I sincerely believed that Brian didn't want Father to drive all the way to the airport.

The straight row of maple trees along the road from Hills Winery to our home had just a few leaves left on their boney branches. The rows of grapevine trees on both sides of the road greeted the wind from the lake with their bare bodies, having lost most of their leaves. But little green leaves fluttered down in the furrows between the grapevines. Although it was already early winter, the radishes stretched out from the ground, baring their naked waist, while the snow-like radish flower blossomed on top of the stalk.

'Father, why are there radishes in the vineyard?'

'The radishes absorb the water the grapevines would. It helps the grapes to be sweeter.'

This was the answer Father gave me, when I asked because I was amazed to see green leaves when all other plants were withering away from the cold. These radishes were late autumn radishes. The late autumn radishes, planted for the sweetening of the grapes, bloomed in the winter, froze, then became nutrients for the grapes.

Not knowing when Brian would arrive, Mother kept her eyes on the winery through the window, while Father kept opening the front door to look at the front yard. The fireplace that Father lit, was slowly warming up the chilly house from the first cold of the winter. Wondering what Brian would look like after three years, curious what kind of person his wife was, I peered out the window pretending not to care.

'Should I make some tea, Mother?"

I asked, while putting on the water for my restless parents. Perhaps I wanted to calm my mind.

'That sounds wonderful. Let's have some tea.'

When Mother walked over to the table from the window, Father nonchalantly sat down saying, "I'm sure they'll arrive some time today." I knew how they felt, restlessly waiting, not knowing when their son would arrive.

As the warm scent of the tea reached our nose, it seemed to calm us down.

"It's warm and nice."

Usually, when Mother saw the bubbles that formed while pouring tea into a cup, she would say, 'Look Anna, it's money!' She would scoop out the bubbles and drink them first, but she seemed to have forgotten that today. Mother told me that Grandmother always enjoyed saying the bubbles were 'money'.

Mother took a sip and closed her eyes. I myself kept looking out to the road full of maple trees even though I was holding a hot cup of tea. The road that would be carrying Brian's car.

All those days that I walked down that road with Brian. Since the day I arrived in this country with my new family to the day that Brian got married, it's been a long time.

I used to walk down the road with Father and Brain waiting for the school bus and after we returned home from school, Father would greet us from the same spot then head for the winery while Brian and I would walk home, joking and laughing. Father built us a small bus stop so we could take shelter when it was raining or snowing. The makeshift shelter still stood so I could reminisce about my childhood once a in a while.

'Dad, We don't need the bus stop anymore.'

'My grandchild will need it.'

When we entered college and didn't need the bus stop anymore, I had a strange idea while listening to the conversation between Brian and Father. That it would be nice if that grandchild was the child that Brian and I would have together. Since Brian was the only man in my mind, it was only fitting that he would be our child.

But that was just the desire of my imagination. The bus stop would one day shelter the children born between Brian Sua, when those children become old enough to attend school.

Even though the limousine that Brian was riding would carry him all the way to the front of the house, my mind was drifting away as I looked out the window.

And that Brian, now husband to another woman, is coming home today. Not knowing when the limousine would arrive, the three of us were trying to calm ourselves with warm tea after restlessly looking out the window without much conversation.

As we were calming our mind with tea, the doorbell rang.

'It's Brian!'

The three of us jumped out of our seats all at once. Father almost threw down the cup on the table and rushed to the door as Mother followed. I stayed a few feet behind as Mother and Father should greet Brian first. My heart felt as if it was about to explode.

"Brian, Sua!"

"Oh, Brian!"

I could see Brian's big smile over Mother and Father's shoulders.

'Brian!'

I called out to Brian in my mind. It was a face I missed.

"Dad, Mom!"

With their luggage still outside, Brian brought in Sua and our parents as Mother weeped.

"Come on in, Sua."

My mother hugged the shoulder of her daughter-in-law that she had never seen before. Sua was a woman with deep eyes, with long dark brown hair draped over her shoulders.

"Oh, Sua, my daughter-in-law!"

Father hugged Sua as soon as Mother let her go. Buried in Father's chest, Sua's eyes were looking at me. For an instant, our eyes met.

"Oh, Anna!"

Just then, Brian, who was standing behind Father and Mother, came and hugged me.

"Brian!"

I lost myself in Brian's arms.

"How are you, Anna?"

Those arms, that chest, the breath, it was the Brian that I remembered. My heart suddenly tightened as my tears swelled about to explode. I shut my eyes trying to prevent exactly that, my tears were already flowing down my cheeks. As I cried in Brian's chest, I noticed Sua's stare as she escaped Father's hug.

Not knowing Sua and I were looking at each other, Brian wiped my tears away. My face felt flushed from Brian's touch. I collected my nerves and walked over to Sua and said, 'Welcome, sua. How was your trip?', grabbing her hand. Her deep dark eyes were like a deep well amidst her soft white skin. I knew Brian had fallen through those deep dark eyes.

I was curious about Brian's wife. Since there wasn't a wedding, it was only natural for me and our parents to be curious.

'Who was she? What kind of a woman would capture Brian's heart?'

It was curiosity as much as an unbearable envy. Brian didn't even take the time to send a picture of her. Me and my parents didn't have a clue who Sua was, furthering our curiosity and disappointment, but we started to piece together the puzzle by looking into her eyes. The piece of the puzzle to what Brian must've liked about her was becoming clear.

"It was good Anna, thanks to Brian."

Sua had just said that the trip was comfortable thanks to Brian. I realized Sua could say anything about Brian, however she wanted. With my heart pounding, I had to be cheerful as Mother and Father.

As Father was busy carrying the four large luggage cases into the house, Mother was getting to know her daughter-in-law with her greeting. 'Welcome Sua.' It was a very noisy reunion.

"The limousine dropped you off in front of the house, right?"

"No, Dad. We actually asked the driver to drop us off at the winery." Brian answered cheerfully as Father's question.

"The wheels did all the work. I wanted to reminisce while walking down the road."

That was Brian's answer to Mother's question, 'You mean to tell me you carried all those luggages?'

Brian smiled as if he became a different person while in Korea and I began to wonder, 'Why did Brian want to reminisce along that road?' I still remembered the time when I heard Brian call out, 'Mommy!' in the darkness of that road and the times when Brian walked to school with me carrying a backpack bigger than himself.

'Anna, wait for me!'

Back then, it was difficult for Brian to carry that backpack walking to and from school because he was a year younger than me. Father would always wait at the bus stop for Brian and I after working at the winery. When we got off the bus, he would alway ask, 'Anna, Brian, did you have fun at school?'. After giving us a hug, he went back to the winery, leaving us to trek down the long road back home.

Brian never had to walk down that road alone. I became his older sister so that he wouldn't have to walk alone.

I was already used to walking in Peru, so I was always a few steps ahead of Brian and he was always behind. I knew the reason Brian was having a hard time in school. It was because of Michael.

'Anna is different, she's different. Why do you live in someone else's house?'

The reason for Michael's bullying as he circled around me was obvious. Even though I couldn't speak or understand English, I knew from Michael's actions and expressions that he was making fun of me. All I could do was kneel on the spot, cover my face, and just listen quietly.

Then, as always, a child suddenly appeared in front of Michael. Brian, who was tender and soft, who couldn't swing a fist, just stood there with his chest huffing and puffing; his face bright red from anger.

'Don't do that to Anna, Michael!'

As Brian clenched his tiny fists, Michael made fun of him too.

'Hey Brian. Why are you so different from Anna?'

I didn't want to go to school because of Michael's bullying, but it wasn't up to me. As long as Brian went to school, I had to go too. In fact, I was able to go to school thanks to Brian.

Since Brian was bullied everyday just as much as me, it must've been difficult for him to walk down the long straight road after we got off the school bus.

One day, I stopped and crouched on the road. I waited for Brian with my arms stretched out backwards.

'What are you doing, Anna?'

Brian stood there bewildered and I had to tell him, 'Get on Brian. Your big sis will carry you.' using my hands and glances.

Brian was shy at first, but he eventually got used to it. He climbed on my back and wrapped his arms around my neck.

'Am I too heavy, Anna? Are you tired?'

Brian kept me company like that.

I understood what he was asking so I tightened my arms and shook my head. In my mind, I was telling him, 'No I'm not. You're not heavy at all. I'm going to give you a piggyback ride everyday.'

One day, while on my back, Brian told me, 'Anna, if Michael bullies you, just say 'No!'. Ok? You got it?' Then he put his hands on the back of my neck, exposed by the pigtails that Mother made me, and put his head on my back and fell asleep. When Brian told me to just say 'No', I just nodded and tightened my arms around him and walked slowly so I could hold him just a bit longer.

Those moments, when I carried Brian home after getting off the school bus, were happier than the ones at school.

And returning home with Sua from Korea, after three years, Brian wanted to walk down that road. Why did he want to walk down that road carrying four luggages even though the limousine could've brought them to the house?

Was it because the road carried his childhood memories? I began to reminisce with sadness.

"Finally, we're all together as a family."

The candles set in the middle of the table for dinner lingered softly. The mood was rather joyful as Brian's favorite food, resting in the silver tray, and the conversation began to blend together. Father lifted his wine glass high and gave a toast, 'Welcome back Brian! Welcome Sua!' Mother and I lifted our wine glasses as well and so began our dinner. Sua, sitting in front of me, seemed very nervous.

"I was disappointed that we couldn't attend the wedding, but this is nice."

Mother expressed her feelings, holding her wine glass. She

must've had a grand plan for her son's wedding so it was understandable that she'd feel disappointed. Brian and Sua kept quiet.

Brian had notified our parents of his wedding over the phone. 'We have our reasons, but Sua and I decided to exchange wedding rings instead of holding a ceremony.'

'I'll tell you when we get home.' That's what Mother told us Brian said.

'I'm so disappointed, Anna. How can Brian do this to us?'

Not knowing the reason and not being able to attend their only son's wedding must've been a huge disappointment.

'I'm sure Brian hasn't forgotten about it.'

Not able to control her feelings, Mother grabbed me and started to cry. She was sure Brian was holding the ceremony without his family because she made sure of the relationship between Brian and I after the incident in the treehouse. But I had a different thought. There had to be a reason why Brian only exchanged rings, instead of a ceremony. Either he was planning a ceremony here at home or there was something with Sua that he was hiding.

Mother tried to lift the mood but Brian just stayed silent and sliced his meat.

"Anna helped me with the dish. She knows your appetite better than I do."

Worried that she might've touched a nerve, Mother changed the subject. That subject was food and I was in it. I already knew of Mother's intentions and I'm sure Brian knew what she was doing as well.

"Thanks Anna. I missed this food!"

Brian said to me.

As soon as I heard Mother say, 'She knows your appetite better than I do,' and Brian saying 'I missed this food', the flood of emotions holding back seemed to burst through my throat.

I pushed down the emotions with a sip of wine and looked towards Sua, who was quietly eating next to Brian. This dinner would've been uneasy for Sua, even without all the pent up emotions between the family members. It was something I experienced as well.

"Anna decorated your room."

Mother again said 'Anna'. I'm sure she was thinking about my feelings in front of Brian and Sua, but it was very uncomfortable to hear. Not understanding how I felt, Father said, 'Is there anything in this house that doesn't have Anna's touch?'

Why were Father and Mother being like this today? I just wanted to grab Sua and disappear. These were things that Sua didn't need to know.

This was a gathering after a long time of waiting.

The dinner was finally over and Brian and Sua went to their room while Mother and Father went to bed.

I opened the window in my room and stood, looking out to Lake Ontario. The moonlight was shining down on the lake. The lake seemed annoyed at the cold air or was it the shining moonlight? Even the lake wanted a quiet night's sleep.

Until now, longing kept me awake, but now the uncertainty of not knowing what to do in this household pushed sleep away. This uncertainty kept nagging me on, asking me if I should leave.

'Leave.'

Why haven't I thought of that before? The thought of always living here with Mother, Father, and Brian had taken root as I got used to this life.

I struggled for a long time to plant my roots in an unfamiliar place, but now I felt it was time to uproot and plant them elsewhere. Facing the strange and unfamiliar was what I feared the most, what I wanted to avoid most, but it seemed the time had come. My heart was like a restless lake in the night.

'Mom!'

Quietly, I called out towards the lake to the mom who didn't exist in this world. The words were Quechua, a sound I was familiar with, but had to be locked away inside me for a long time.

'Mario!'

Did my brother Mario know I would someday feel like this? Was this why he tried to stop our Father?

'Wherever Mamani is going, you and I aren't there!'

These were the words Mario said as he stood up to Father's pleading.

My life was now saying, 'Let's leave', without an idea of when and where to go. So my heart was like a lake in the night.

'Mom!'

I was calling out to the mom who wouldn't answer.

I was being swallowed by my thoughts. It was no wonder I couldn't go to sleep.

4. Brian and I

I feel awkward, even at my own home, as if I'm a guest who has overstayed their welcome. I felt like I was trapped at a dead end and thoughts of leaving just contributed more to my sleepless nights. Afraid I might slip up when looking at Brian or talking to Sua, I was always on edge.

Did I really need to go back to my homeland, Peru?

There wasn't any family there to welcome me back and to be honest, my homeland seemed more foreign now than when I first came to Canada. Wherever it might be, if I were to go there, I needed to leave this house first. This was best for me and the whole family.

I was envious of how Brian just decided to leave for Korea with luggage three years ago. Now that my mind was set, I decided to pack my bags and tell my parents.

'You are my daughter, Anna.'

After what she saw that day, Mother might have regretted adopting me. Because we started as siblings, we should've been siblings to the end, but that day was a betrayal to the ends of the root.

However, there was something that Father and Mother overlooked as well. The fact that children grow up in mind and body together. That while the body can grow on its own, the mind grows towards each other. When two people want to bond with each other, their feelings for each other are stronger than any boundaries. Ever since Brian was six years old and I was seven, it was a feeling that arose from being within just reach of one another.

Brian and I weren't reckless or faithful to our feelings, because we suffered teetering on the line between desire and repression. The root of trust, dependence and consideration for each other since our childhood was the foundation that kept us restrained whenever we were about to cross the boundary.

The fact that Brian was able to confide in me with his nightmares during his teenage years, while not being able to talk to our parents, was proof of how much we trusted and depended on each other even as we struggled between childhood and adulthood. Just as Brian comforted me with my struggles with unfamiliarity when I was young, I tried to share the weight of Brian's awful memories with him. We tried to uncover, listen, and care for each other's pain. This was our love, formed between Brian and I, stronger than our desires.

Our Mother was worried that our mind and bodies would cross the boundary, but we kept ourselves in check in our own way by sharing our feelings. That's how we made our way to adulthood from our childhood.

I can now tell the story. The story that only Brian and I know. The horrific memory that's deeply engraved in Brian's heart, the events that led me to become Brian's older sister, and our journey to maturity.

As always, I was playing the zamponya in the treehouse that day. The late spring breeze that brushed the surface of Lake Ontrario blew in through the open window and the clear silhouette of the CN Tower at the end of the lake told me the weather was clear and bright.

I was reminiscing about my brother Mario and my Father as I played 'The Lonely Shepherd' that Mario used to play. It had been a long time since I flew far away to this foreign country and when I received word that my brother had died in prison while my Father passed away, drunk on chicha, in tears alone.

As I played 'The Lonely Shepherd' while reminiscing about my brother and Father, something gently weighed down on my shoulders.

I kept playing as Brian leaned down on me.

'Anna!'

Brian calling out to me, while leaning on my shoulders, sounded like a moan. I quickly removed my lips from the zamponya.

'What is it Brian?

I could tell what Brian was feeling by the tone and the sound of his breath.

Brian's eyes were already overflowing with tears as I spun around and looked into his eyes.

'Brian!'

I comforted him as I wiped his tears that fell and rolled down his

cheeks.
'I feel like dying!'
'Are you sick?'
I felt a sudden jolt of fear as if my foot slipped off a high ledge. Even though we've always been together since childhood and even though I knew what Brian was feeling just by listening to the sound of his breath, I had no idea as to the reason why he felt like dying.
'I'm scared!'
Brain buried his face into my bosom. Cold sweat was running down his face. Like if he was being chased by something.
'It's alright Brian. It's okay. I'm here.'
I hugged Briana and rubbed down his back. Shivering in my arms, Brian was like a six year old child. I waited for Brian to tell me all his fears as I patted his back.
When I was seven and Brian six years old, we were like a fork and a knife, one to cut and the other to grab and bring it to the mouth. The fork knew the nature of the knife and the knife knew the fork as much as itself, so they were able to become one even though they looked different.
First, I stayed true to my role as a sister, but my heart gradually began to take the lead. By the time my heart was full with my desires, there was no need to be conscious of my role. It was already all in my mind. It was the same with Brian. When I was always in tears because of this unfamiliar place, Brian was by my side as if only he could comfort me. He dried my eyes and made me laugh out loud.
I thought we knew each other by heart, but that's when Brian said that he felt like dying and that he was afraid. I felt like it was my fault, caused by my carelessness that I thought I knew everything about Brian. Something that I didn't know, this fear existed in Brian.
'I'm sorry, Brian, I didn't know how you felt.'
I said to myself as I stroked through Brian's hair and patted his back.
Brian stayed in my arms then called out to me, 'Anna', then gently pushed me aside and started talking.
'I was riding my bicycle in the yard that day. Mom was probably in the backyard.'
Brian looked out the window towards Lake Ontario. I was holding Brian's hand.
'Someone suddenly came out of nowhere and hugged me, saying,

'Come with me baby.' I was so scared that I couldn't even cry. I yelled out, 'Mommy', but she didn't come. The Man grabbed me, put me in his car, and started to drive off. That's when I realized what was happening and started to cry out loud. Mom still didn't come.'

'Brian, you?'

'Yeah.'

Goosebumps ran down my spine.

I sat Brian down in a chair and I sat next to him.

'Don't ever leave Brian alone, Anna.'

That's what Mother always told me even in the plane coming over from Peru. I finally knew what she meant. This was the reason I couldn't leave Brian alone and the reason I became his older sister.

'He told me, 'Your mom won't come if you cry.' and took me to the basement of a house. I couldn't cry out of fear and repeatedly woke up, thinking of my mom. Why wasn't she next to me while I was being taken by a scary stranger? Why wasn't she coming for me? Then one night, it must've been very late at night, he put me in his car and took me somewhere. He told me, 'I'm sorry child for what I put you through. But you saved my child.' Then he let me out of his car.'

Brian's hand was soaking wet.

'He whispered to me, 'See those lights over there? That's where your mom and dad are waiting for you. I'll stay here. You cry out loud for your mom and dad. Run towards the lights as you cry out for them. So your mom will hear you."

He told me he couldn't take a single step towards the pitch black darkness, but with the Man reassuring Brian that 'he'll stay here', Brian was able to step out into the darkness, calling for him mom.

'I was even more scared that he'd leave me there. He kept urging me, 'Cry louder so your mom can hear you.' and at that moment, I believed him more than my mom who wasn't next to me. Mom who didn't know I disappeared. Mom who didn't come for me when I was trapped in the basement. But all I could do was cry out for her.'

'Brian!'

I wrapped my arms around Brian.

'I walked towards the light, falling again and again, shouting 'Mommy'. Then I heard my mom calling out, 'Brian, my baby!' It really was her. That's how I was able to go back home. I never heard that Man's voice ever again. This was when I was five years old.'

This was the memory of Brian's kidnapping.
'I remembered what he said to me, everything I went through. But when mom and dad asked me what happened, I couldn't say a word. I wanted to, but nothing came out.'
Even after his voice came back, he lived in fear because he was too afraid of remembering.
Then, on their usual family trip, this time to Peru, he met a little girl named Mamani and she became Anna. Even though our parents never said so, perhaps it was all meticulously planned, disguised as an ordinary trip. It was their way of adopting me, without Brian realizing it, so the two of us could grow up naturally as siblings.
'What happened back then, they're starting to show up in my dreams. I call out for mom in that dark basement but my voice won't come out. He tells me to call out to mom and walk towards the light, but I can't move.'
The nightmare was manifesting in Brian's dreams, unable to call out and unable to move.
'Do you think he was a kidnapper or just a father trying to save his child? Why can't I erase my resentment towards mom?'
When Brian revealed the weight of his nightmare, I was disappointed that I was still a teenager just like Brian. If I was an adult, just a little bit more thoughtful and a bit wiser, I would've been able to lessen his burden but nothing of the sort came to my mind.
'Brian, that man abducted a little child.'
I spoke softly.
'He did a very bad thing to a child and put our parents through unspeakable pain. He wronged you, and our parents, so he needs to answer for your nightmares.'
I wanted to put Brian's mind at ease so that the nightmares would never disturb him again, but I didn't know how.
'You're all right now Brian. You let everything go, so it's okay.'
This was how Brian comforted me when I had to start a new life after being adopted. He was always on my side, at my side. Just as I was able to free myself from the unfamiliarity, Brian needed to be free from his nightmares.
'Why didn't I realize that mom must've suffered because she lost me?' Brian said. He must've realized how Mother felt back then. It marked the beginning of healing between Mother and Brian.

‘You were weighed down with this nightmare for so long.’

Brian nodded. He was a good kid.

He was on his way to being free from his nightmares and the resentment towards our Mother.

We protected each other, while teetering on the boundary, and I became a woman and Brian, a young man.

When our minds grew along with our bodies, our parents were worried about the possibility that two young hearts might commit, but we were able to get free from the nightmares by sharing the weight of our silent past. We were learning to deal with the deep rooted resentment as well.

This was the relationship between Brian and I, and it was our way of love.

5. Torture and Wet Fire Log

Brian immersed himself working at the winery as if he needed to fill his three year absence. In my eyes, he looked like someone who had let go of his past.

Sua, with her deep eyes, was cautious and quiet like a shadow; perhaps because of the unfamiliarity. Still, it seemed like she was quietly talking to me alot.

Sua's ambiguous looks seemed to be saying that she wanted to be friendly with me. Other times, her looks seemed to say, 'I know all about your relationship with Brian.'

But I was wrestling with myself every day, trying to root out the deep feelings for Brian since I was a child, and trying to figure out when and where to leave.

Looking back now, ever since I came here with my new parents and we became a family, it was fate that Brian and I became close as much as we did. The reason for my adoption was for Brian to not be alone anymore. It was something that our parents and my Peruvian Father arranged, without any consent from me or Brian. If I had said, 'I don't want to father', would I still be living in Peru? Being a child, I had to do what the adults told me to and Brian was too young.

Whether at home or at school, wherever Brian was, I had to be there with him. From spring to early fall, it wasn't strange to see Brian lying on my lap reading a book or for me to knit or play the zamponya while Brian rested on my lap in the treehouse. As we grew up together and even though our breaths grew closer and closer in the treehouse, we were always together.

Sometimes Brian would take off the ladder as a joke and would climb the tree. So I learned to climb trees as well. Mother hated it when we moved the ladder because she couldn't bring us any snacks. I'm sure she had an idea why Brian was moving the ladder. Brian was fast becoming a young man, while I was becoming a woman day by day.

Brian already knew that bringing snacks was Mother's way of keeping her eyes on us. There was tension between a mother and a son over a ladder, but it was impossible to separate the two of us because we had already become close since childhood.

I spent most of my time in the treehouse while Brian was away for three years. When he suddenly left saying, 'I won't be long', I believed he would come back just as suddenly calling out, 'Anna!' If there was no waiting, those three years would've been time I slowly died.

It was love that was nervously built over and over again as if walking on a tightrope, but it seemed like Sua was staring at me with those deep eyes as if I was overflowing with emotions.

But I had to hide my emotions, fighting with myself, acting and smiling like the good daughter and the older sister that I was. I needed to speak more often and laugh louder for Sua who must've been uneasy, for our parents who trusted me, and for Brian who must've been uncomfortable between Sua and I.

I realized, having to speak and laugh casually could be torture.

A calm excitement began to fill the once quiet house, regardless of my feelings, after Brian and Sua arrived.

The house became alive with Brian's voice and Father and Mother couldn't keep quiet, catching up with Brian and Sua. Brian seemed unusually upbeat and happy, as if he was trying to confirm his existence after a three year absence. Perhaps it was a gesture of concern for Sua and her unfamiliarity or for me, who would feel awkward between Brian and Sua.

Sua was so calm and quiet just like her deep eyes that Father and Mother kept circling around her so they could find a chance to talk to her. I watched as my parents hovered around Sua like a child curious about a new family member.

Mother and Father spoke to Sua often, worried that she might feel left out in the family conversation due to her language barrier, but Sua spoke English well. To be able to speak a native language meant overcoming one of the obstacles that Sua might've first encountered and would follow her to the end.

But when I was seven, when I came to this country with my new parents, I didn't know how to speak English. I spoke Quechua along with my father, mother, and brother. Almost half the population were Quechua. Machu Picchu, the City of The Sun, was Quechua for Old Peak.

A seven year old, who spoke only that language, living in a foreign country in a new house with new parents was stress itself. The more my new kind mother, father, and young Brian hovered around me to talk to me, I felt afraid and teary, not knowing where to lean. Since I didn't know how to communicate with my new family, I had no choice but to keep my mouth shut. I didn't know how to express the feeling of shrinking inward from fear and tension.

Brian followed me around like my shadow and kept talking to me, as if he knew how I felt. He would be asleep at my bedside when I woke up and tried to talk to me, worried that I might cry.

'Good morning, Anna! Anna, try saying Good morning to me too,' Brian would say, pointing to himself with his cute little hand. He was a lovely child.

My tense, sad heart that shrank inward began to soften little by little thanks to Brian's babbling as he followed me around. I found myself always next to Brian because I found him to be my windshield. To be always with Brian, that was the purpose of my adoption.

Mother and Father put me in the same school as Brian so that I could be an older sister to him, but back then, it was Brian who was taking care of me. Most of my English lessons were from Brian.

That was me, but seeing as how Sua spoke English pretty well, it didn't seem like she'd have any trouble with language barriers. Brian said that he met her at an English class, so he must've taught her just as he taught me. And love blossomed between the two.

While Brian was teaching Sua and love was growing between them in Korea, not knowing what was happening, I neglected my growing feelings for Brian. If there was no waiting as my feelings burned inside me, I probably would've withered to death from the bitter longing. How painful it must've been for Mother, recalling the old memories. Brian, himself, was the pain for Mother and I that no one could have ever imagined.

For Mother, Brian's absence was the cause of her guilt and remorse. She believed, Brian's absence was due to her carelessness and stubbornness. It was her carelessness that saw her young son be kidnapped that spring and also the reason that Brian left for Korea.

'What if he doesn't come, Anna?'

Mother became very anxious after Brian left for Korea.

'He'll come back. He said he won't take long.'

I didn't know when that would be, but I had no choice but to reassure Mother. I was only able to overcome the endless waiting by repeating Brian's words like prayer to comfort Mother and myself.

'You're right. He'll come. He found his way in the dark back then... It was hell back then, Anna.'

I knew what she was talking about. It was when Brian had been abducted. I had heard it from Brian, the child that Mother had lost.

'I can't forgive myself when I think of how I lived day to day, imagining the hell that Brian went through.'

Then she brought up the nightmare that she must have hidden as deep as Brian.

'It was a nice day. The sun was exceptionally bright. Everyone was tired from the long winter. Brian was riding his bike in the front yard. I was doing laundry in the backyard and forgot that Brian was playing alone in the front yard because it was so sunny. While basking in the warm sun, I suddenly remembered that Brian was alone. I went to the front yard to play with him, but Brian wasn't there. Only his bike. I called out for him and looked all over the house, the vineyard, but he was nowhere to be found. I didn't know what to do. I barely brought myself to call your father. Tom, the police, 911, hurry! This is how people go crazy.'

But Father wanted to search a bit longer before calling the police. They were searching the basement when a call came. It was from the Man who took Brian.

'The Man on the phone said, "I have your child. Five thousand dollars. My child is very sick. Don't worry about your child. If you call the police, my, my child, and your child will die." His voice was shaking so much that it was as if he was the one who had lost a child.'

Father was trembling as he listened to the Man who took their child for five thousand dollars and Mother fainted with the receiver still in her hand.

'I yelled out on the floor, 'Five thousand dollars, five thousand dollars, Tom. Hurry!' and your father grabbed me and said, 'Joanne, you need to calm down so Brian can survive.' He was crying and it drove us crazy knowing that we couldn't go to the police and there was no other way to save our son.'

It wasn't even fifty thousand, but five thousand dollars. How were they supposed to deliver the money? Father didn't know what to do when the Man called again and told Father where to drop off the money. He reiterated not to tell anybody or everyone would die.

'All we could do was wait with the money for the instructions and do you know what your Father said? 'His child seems to be seriously ill. He must've done this out of panic, so let's try appealing to a father's compassion. A father's compassion? Does it make sense to expect father's compassion from a kidnapper? I wanted to rip his mouth wide open right then and there.'

Mother was furious as if she'd really do it if Father was in front of her, even though this happened long ago because her anger and desperation still remained.

'If you think about it, there was nothing we could really do. He was threatening to kill Brian if we went to the police, so what can your Father do? It was my fault for losing myself in the sunlight while my son was being taken away. The four days I spent on the patio was true hell. It was on the fourth day out on the patio that I heard it. Someone calling out mommy. I thought it was a dream or a hallucination, but then your Father said to me, 'Joanne, do you hear it?' If I was alone, I would've thought I was hallucinating, but your Father was hearing it too. We both ran towards the sound. We ran in the darkness through the winery, stumbling and falling, as the sound grew louder. Then we saw him. Our little Brian coming towards us, crying and falling. I grabbed Brian from the darkness and just cried out... 'Oh God!'

Mother said the night was too dark to recognize the Man who kidnapped Brian even if he was standing right in front of them.

Just like Brian, who had suffered waiting for Mother to save him down in that basement, Mother also suffered from the horrible memories of losing her only son. Longing for the son who grew up and ran away to Korea from a forbidden love, Mother had brought out the nightmare that she wanted to erase forever.

'Anna, I raised you two and brother and sister. That's how it started so that's what we knew. But there was something that I didn't see. That... feeling. The feeling that naturally grew while growing up together, I didn't expect it, so I didn't understand it.'

Still, Mother never forgot to say that she expected us to live as siblings.

Mother and Father seemed to be relieved because to them, Sua was the absolute boundary, more so than a hundred requests from Mother.

'Sua, tell us about Brian in Korea.'

Mother had lots of questions, so when Father and Brian left for the winery, she asked Sua about Brian. How the two met, what Brian's life was like in Korea, if he seemed happy. The questions were out of curiosity about Brian in Korea, but this was also Mother's way of involving Sua in our family.

In reality, Mother knew nothing about Brian's three years in Korea. When Brian occasionally called, Mother couldn't put down the phone in hopes of hearing more of her son's voice, but all Brian gave her was a short simple greeting.

I think it was Brian acting like a child, grumbling and acting up out of revenge. Still, it was a way of emotional communication that was only possible between a mother and a child.

'He was a playful teacher.'

Sua brought up Brian's playfulness first. I thought she was going to tell Mother about Brian's everyday life in Korea.

'Brian does have a playful side, doesn't he Anna?'

Mother looked at me and winked.

I thought she might've brought up the memory of the ladder. The times when Brian moved the ladder so Mother wouldn't be able to climb up to the tree house.

Brian hated the basement. No, he feared it due to his traumatic past.

Until then, however, the basement was an entertainment space for the whole family. There was a wine bar where our parents could enjoy wine, a TV and stereo, and toys for Brian. It was a space where the whole family could rest after a hard day's work.

The basement had a door that connected directly to the backyard. When you opened the door, you could see Lake Ontario right in front of your eyes and came out to the backyard where you could enjoy barbeque and wine in the summer while enjoying the lakeview. The basement would've been a great place to hang out had it not been for the kidnapping. So when Brian was fearful of going down the basement, Father built a treehouse on top of the oak tree overlooking Lake Ontario. This wasn't long after I came to live with my new family.

When my Father built the treehouse, he made a window so that we could look down at Lake Ontario located below the hill and Mother brought us chairs and a table so we could read books. Father placed a removable ladder so that Brian and I could climb up and down the tree without the ladder when we grew up. He was letting children be children.

When Brian and I became old enough to climb the tree, Brian sometimes took off the ladder and we'd climb to the treehouse, but Mother hated it. Mother used to say it was dangerous for us to climb without the ladder, but really, it was because she couldn't bring us snacks to keep an eye on us as we grew up.

When Brian learned of Mother's intentions, he removed the ladder and climbed up and down like a squirrel and I was already used to climbing trees.

How could I not know about Brian's playfulness that annoyed Mother so much because he wanted to be with me? I remember all of his pranks that Mother didn't know of.

From the time Brian and I were old enough to walk by ourselves without Father waiting for us at the bus stop, we would walk home along the maple road.

Brian would sometimes fall to the ground while walking. A kid who was smaller and weaker than me, was now taller and a man.

'Anna, get on my back. It's my turn now!'

'No, I'm not a baby Brian.'

As Brian sat there and waited for me with his arms outstretched behind him, I pushed him away.

'We're not going home until you get on Anna!' Brian just sat in the middle of the road, being stubborn as always.

'I'm not you, Brian. You were a kid back then.'

'I want to give you a piggyback ride Anna. If you don't get on, I'm going to carry you.'

He stood up and started to chase me. As I ran around, trying not to get caught, I kind of thought I wanted to get on his back. To get on his back and whisper in his ear, 'Am I heavy? Are you tired?' and rest my face on his big broad shoulders.

Brian's thin voice was already deepening and his face was becoming home to few pimples. Brian pretended not to, but he kept brushing his hand on my body and gazed at me without the familiar baby-like innocence, instead with an unfamiliar heat. We didn't know it at the time, but we were already dangerously close to crossing the boundary set by our parents as brother and sister.

If it wasn't for Brian's pranks, I can't imagine how we could've kept our boundary. Pulling pranks on each other, that was how we showed our love for each other.

Sua's deep eyes were twinkling to suggest she was ready to tell Mother everything even if she didn't ask more questions.

'I looked forward to class. Brian made everyone laugh.'

Sua must've seen Brian's side that made people laugh. I suddenly felt jealous, as if Sua had taken away the only thing that Brian and I had between us because I laughed the most thanks to Brian.

'The first time we had coffee was at the academy cafe.'

Sua's eyes told everyone that she was at the beginning of their love. Her always deep and quiet eyes, now twinkling, and her eager lips wanting to show her burning feelings, I knew these were the expressions of a person who embraced love because that was me at one point in time.

Sua now wanted to say everything, but I had nothing to say.

Suddenly, I wanted to burn up my love that wasn't able to burn like a wet fire log that brought out only bitter tears with the flames of love that Sua was showing. I wanted to burn it all down and turn it into ashes. So that the name Brian wouldn't be a sorrowful pain and I can look at him as my younger brother.

'And?'

Mother was already caught up in Brian and Sua's love story. Mother who was wary of my love for Brian.

'Brian began to tell me about Canada... No, this town. About the lake, fishing, orchard, and the treehouse. He would tell me about one thing everyday and say, 'Tomorrow', then went to class. But there was one thing he would always include in his stories. His family. You, father, and especially his older sister, Anna.'

Listening to Brian and Sua's love story, I needed to burn away the wet firewood that failed to burn properly in my heart, leaving me with only pain, then Sua said it. His older sister Anna was always in his stories.

'Talked about his older sister, Anna, everyday...'

The wet firewood inside me began to smoke without fire, stinging my eyes. Causing tears to swell from deep within. Bewildered, I didn't know what to do as tears started to fill my eyes, as Mother looked at me.

'Brian didn't say anything bad about me, did he?'

Mother suddenly cut in, trying to keep Sua from noticing me.

'Of course not. Brian said that your cooking is great and that his sister's cooking is great too because she learned from her mother. He said you two make the best roast beef and meat pie so I began to take interest in cooking as well.' Sua smiled. The expression on her face, as she talked about their love, was innocent.

'Brian said his older sister played the zamponya really well. He said that listening to his sister play made him calm and want to cry sometimes. So I became interested in zamponya. It was an instrument I've never heard of.' As soon as I heard Sua's words, an agonizing pain passed right through my chest.

The fact that Brian wanted to cry was proof that he was suffering from longing even if he had left for Korea after feeling frustrated from Mother's opposition to our uncontrollable love.

'I gave Brian the nickname, Scheherazade, because he told me a story everyday.'

Mother looked at me as if asking what Sua meant, so I told her, 'She was a woman who told a king one story every night for a thousand days to save her own life, and became a queen.'

'So you mean that our Brian told one story every day like that lady to win Sua's heart?' Mother laughed.

'Isn't our Brian a romantic, Anna?'

It meant that from then on, Brian's heart began to pull towards Sua.

Part of my heart began to ach once more. But I needed to feel more pain. So that the fire of their love would burn all the love in me. Was Sua alway this talkative? Sua spoke so well, but I had to keep my mouth shut even if I had many things I wanted to say.

'Then one day, Brian said he wouldn't be Scheherazade any more.'

Sua suddenly created tension from her carefully unfolding love story by throwing out a plot twist.

'Why all of a sudden?' Mother and I asked by looking into Sua's deep eyes. Looking into those eyes, I thought, Sua was someone who knew how to maximize the effect of a story.

'I thought it was over between us. I felt sad thinking I couldn't speak to Brian anymore. To be honest, I was also going through some rough times and talking to Brian helped me.'

Even though Sua briefly brought up her personal story, Mother and I couldn't show any interest. All I could think about was how Brian had already noticed Sua's pain and was trying to help her heal in his own way. It was Brian that I knew.

The first time Brian noticed how I felt and comforted me was when I came here and became a member of an unfamiliar family and I was always in tears because there was nothing to relate to.

Brian always liked to put his hand out in front of me whenever I sat silently with my face in my laps. In his hand was a cookie or a candy that Mother had made.

'Let's share.'

Even though I was a child, I knew those words meant 'I'm by your side.' Those actions were Brian's warm intentions disguised as cookies and candies. And his intentions became a force whenever Michael bullied me in school.

So, it wasn't difficult for me to imagine that Brian's kindness would heal and open up Sua's heart.

'Why do you suppose Brian stopped being Scheherazade?' Mother asked, unable to contain her curiosity and urged Sua.

'Brian said that love isn't a game where you bet your life on it. He wanted to love in his own way.'

Mother's eyes began to twinkle with curiosity.

'Love in his own way...'

While Mother's eyes twinkled with gladness, I was caught up in what Brian had said. Because his words meant it was love for Sua.

A fire ignited within me and started to burn.

'Was Sua testing me right now, on purpose?'

It was as if Sua was testing me, saying that I needed to burn up the unrestrained jealousy first, before burning the love that failed to burn before from my tears.

'And he said, 'Come to Canada with me, Sua.''

'Oh my, that's a proposal!'

Mother suddenly clapped and shouted as tears swelled up in her eyes.

'Come to Canada with me, Sua.'

Sua must've wanted to say this. That's why she suddenly created tension with a plot twist and raised me and Mother's curiosity.

Well, Sua sure did succeed. Mother was filled with tears of joy from her son's story and I was engulfed with flames of jealousy and pain.

With my jealousy burning hotter than the flames of their love, and with this miserable heart of mine, I wanted to shout please stop, but my hands and feet were tied up. My heart felt like it would become a graveyard of ashes, If I left my words, hands, and feet to burn like this.

This was actually my own fault. Teetering on the boundary, I should've tried to cross it at least once, but all I thought about was that the boundary was drawn by Mother. What was more stubborn than Mother's boundary was the limits I set on myself. It was my fault that Brian, who was about to cross, turned around.

How could Brian believe in me, I who collapsed in fear, and insisted on Brian to change our parents' minds on his own? In spite of this, the jealousy within me that burned like fire was the inevitable price of unrequited love. So I needed to burn everything that had to be burned, so that my heart could become a graveyard of cold ashes.

'Isn't our Brian such a romantic, Anna?'

Mother again pulled me into her own admiration. My mother, who didn't have any care for my feelings, was looking like a girl who fell in love for the first time.

Forgetting to answer, I was lost in thought with a sad heart. I wanted to find a way to say goodbye to my first love before my love for him burned up into cold ashes. And to bury it deep in my heart and leave this place.

6. Dawn's Farewell Ceremony

The long winter in Ontario deepened. Even when the plants rooted in the ground were swayed by the cold wind that swept the lake, there was a particularly upright group.
When all the trees stood alone individually, there was a group that held together branch by branch to live and die together. They were grapevines. Every day, as wind gusts blew and snow covered their feet, the grapevines stood firm.

The dark winter sky color of Lake Ontario could not turn white no matter how much snow fell on it. On a windy day, when water from a far rushed in succession and slammed the hill in front of the house with all its might then collapsed on the spot, Lake Ontario finally vomited white bubbles.

However, as winter deepened, our house became warmer and brighter. The fireplace kept the temperature of the house warm by turning on and off by itself. The news that Sua was pregnant made the atmosphere in the house even warmer. The baby was due in late summer.

"Don't forget, Brian. It's tomorrow morning."
Father once more loudly reminded Brian of the grape harvest at early dawn tomorrow morning. Even if Brian didn't go, the workers would've taken care of the harvest themselves, but Brian has been participating in the winter harvest with the workers for several years already. It was because I urged him to participate.

Around the time the grapes were making their own sweetness, the workers would harvest grapes as they froze and thawed in a net set along the vines. Brian planned to join them in the early morning as the owner of the winery.

"Anna, you're going too, right?"

At father's words, Brian looked back at me for a moment.

But I couldn't answer. Because it wasn't the time to impulsively follow Brian anymore.

I knew why Brian turned to look at me. Before Brian went to Korea, we always waited for this day at this time of the year to harvest the grapes along with the workers. Father and Mother tried to talk us out of it saying it was cold, but I urged Brian. It was because I wanted to be next to Brian. The job entailed putting on several layers of clothing, thick gloves, a headlamp, and harvesting frozen grapes in the early morning.

"One year, in November, the temperature dropped to minus 10 and 11 degrees, but we still needed to harvest. It was fantastic. It was before the flocks of birds arrived and we could avoid the bad weather so we were able to harvest more."

Father said it was the first time in 30 years of vineyard farming. When the weather lasts from minus 8 to 12 degrees for three days, it's time to harvest. During this time, the ripe grapes are frozen and thawed, and as they're frozen again, the sweetness concentrates in the grapes.

Usually, grapes were efficiently harvested by machines, but winter grapes were done by hand. And since the grapes were frozen, they had to be squeezed using a compressor to get the juice.

Even though I was picking grapes in the early morning with the tips of my nose and ears frozen and my fingers numb, my heart was burning hot. It was because Brian was by my side. We laughed and pretended not to but leaned on each other and felt each other as we picked grapes. Sometimes, even the sound of our laughter froze in the cold because our mouths froze. It was a job that we couldn't do for long due to the cold, but Brian and my heart were stronger than the bitter cold.

Not being able to ignore the annual harvesting, Brian had to go and that was why he looked at me and I didn't nod. The reason for me to go had disappeared. There was no reason for me to risk my limbs freezing and my body turning into a snowman in the cold. Because Brian was no longer my Brian.

"Aren't you going, Anna?"

When I didn't answer, Father asked again. It was him asking why I wasn't going when Brian was going. To Father, it was natural for me to

go where Brian went.
'Brian and I, sure it was natural. But why am I hesitating now?'
The moment I asked myself, my mind suddenly started to sway saying, 'Yeah, lets go, just like before.' Even though he was no longer my Brian, that didn't mean I had to avoid him. I was his older sister, so I'd be going with my brother.
"I'll go, Father."
I suddenly replied cheerfully.
Maybe the reason my parents didn't mind that Brian and I went back to harvesting together was because, even if they erased the boundary they created between Brian and I, the existence of Sua acted as a clear boundary.
The wind had fallen asleep at dawn in the arms of the lake, as the surroundings were calm. When we reached the farm, the workers were already standing along the furrow.
"Good morning!"
As Brian greeted the workers who arrived first and were waiting, the workers, who would normally now be waking up, responded, 'Good morning!' The darkness was illuminated by the headlamps of the workers. Me, Brian and the workers, dressed as thick as snowmen, stood in front of a round wooden barrel.
"Shall we begin?"
As soon as Brian spoke, the workers put their barrels close to the vines and carefully raised the nets and began to pick the frozen grapes. The amount of grapes for icewine was very small in quantities compared to the regular grape harvest, so icewine was more precious and expensive.
In early spring, while standing along the procession of vines, the workers are usually talkative when pruning or tying the branches. But when harvesting grapes for icewine, everyone is silent. It's probably because of the cold in the early morning. With their hands stiff and their mouths freezing cold, even if they say something, the sound that escaped their mouth would freeze.
The grape clusters that had been frozen in the snow for several days were heavy. Grapes that ripened in the autumn sunlight would've had a deeper taste and aroma, as they were repeatedly frozen and thawed.
I rolled the net, picked the grapes, and put them in a barrel.
The net was used to protect the grapes from birds.

Flocks of birds always showed up right before the autumn harvest. They would fly around the vineyard and pick the sweet grapes from the branches. A Bird Banger was installed to scare away the birds by regularly playing gunshot sounds, but the birds had already been accustomed to the sound and they would just fly down and enjoy the sweet grapes. Just as the vineyards were endless, the birds too seem to be endlessly flying over the frozen grapes, waiting to be harvested.

Brian and I kept moving our numbing hands to pick the grapes and put them in the barrel.

"It's cold, huh Anna?"

"It's not that bad."

I kept my focus on the grapes as I felt Brian's breath.

"Are you going to be okay?"

Even though there was nothing to worry about before when Brian and I slurred words in the cold while picking grapes, today Brian was concerned about me.

"It's not the first time. I'm fine, Brian."

Because this wasn't my first time, I told him I wasn't cold. I was very formal. I got the feeling Brian was looking at me, but I pretended not to notice.

At one point I turned my head and I saw Brian's eyes looking at me through the shining light of my head-lamp. I was pretty sure that Brian was uncomfortable with me talking so formally.

'What should I do, Brian?'

I was thinking to myself, ignoring Brian's gaze, focusing my hands and eyes on the grapes. I felt Brian doing nothing. He was just looking at me quietly with his hand on the grapes in the net.

I couldn't handle Brian's gaze, so I stubbornly focused on the grapes in front of me. The frozen grapes dangling in the net wouldn't come out quickly. It looked like a bunch had been caught between the nets. Maybe it wasn't the net, but my mind that was tangled. My tangled heart must have been frozen like the grapes caught in the net.

"I'm sorry, Anna."

Brian said as he brought down his hand from the grapes. He must've thought I was lashing out at the frozen grapes because I couldn't control my feelings. It wasn't false.

So many things I wanted to say were piled up in my heart, but there wasn't any way to let them out. I was already speechless because of

Sua, but I still had to laugh and have a friendly conversation, feeling like the frozen grapes trapped in a net.

Brian was just looking at me, with the frozen grapes in front of him just waiting.

"Don't be sorry, Brian."

I said, with my eyes on the grapes that wouldn't escape from the net. It was nobody's fault, so I couldn't blame anyone. The aftermath of an unsuccessful love will heal over time, but we must understand each other's unfamiliar faces during that time, because we are paying the price of love.

"I'm sorry, I'm really sorry..."

Brian kept apologizing. It was the first time Brian whispered after returning with Sua from Korea.

"We're going our separate ways. In time, everything will be fine."

Although this was what I was saying, this whole situation was unfamiliar to me too. This situation where Brian told me he was sorry, I never wanted to make Brian feel sorry towards me, and I never thought he should be sorry to me, but this strange situation I was forced to face was something I've been afraid of since I was a child. So the feeling of 'unfamiliar', which I wanted to avoid, was more terrifying. I wanted to get out of this situation.

"I'm leaving, Brian."

I revealed my carefully planned intentions. I was planning to tell my parents first, but this uncomfortable situation had caused me to reveal my thoughts.

Truthfully, there were enough reasons for me to become independent. I didn't want Brian and Sua to feel uncomfortable because of me and neither did I. And I was old enough to be independent.

"No you can't, Anna!"

Brian shouted out loud, and grabbed my shoulder with his gloved hand. The head-lamp lights on our heads lit each other's faces. Brian's expression reflected in my head-lamp seemed to be very angry or dumbfounded. The workers were already ahead of us, harvesting their shares.

"I'm old enough to live alone now..."

"If you leave, I'm leaving too!"

"..!"

Brian cut me off as if he was waiting. And it was as if Brian put a gag in my mouth when he said, 'I'm leaving too!'

Brian's eyes reflected in my head-lamp were as determined as his voice. It was just like Brian when left for Korea with his big backpack.

'Then what should I do, Brian?'

I asked Brian with my eyes. At that moment, the image of Brian leaving the house with his large backpack flashed in front of my eyes. And the image of Mother, weeping as she sent her son away, followed.

I knew Brian never talked nonsense. If he said he was leaving the house, then he was really leaving.

Where had our warm hearts gone, those times when we picked frozen grapes along the vines, laughing and playing in the bitter cold that swept Lake Ontario? It made it sad that words like 'sorry' and 'leaving' hung over us with the cold. I didn't like the fact that the memories that I thought had burned to ashes were still here, making Brian heated. It's true I was thinking about when and where I would go, but I wasn't planning on telling Brian.

"I'm going to go home, Brian. Is that alright?"

I said as I looked into Brian's eyes shining in my headlamp and as Brian held onto my shoulders. I felt I needed to go home so Brian could resume work along with the workers, since he was the owner.

"No! Don't go. Don't do that, Anna."

I thought he was going to tell me to go home because it was cold, and I would feel uncomfortable, but what he said was, 'No!' The moment he told me not to go, I became confused and looked at Brian.

I had never been used to going against Brian, at least until now and except for the time I caused him to leave for Korea. It was the same with Brian.

"Anna, tell me you're not leaving! Promise me you'll never say that again!"

Brian was urging me. As if he was trying to force me.

Brian's stubbornness. The stubbornness that I remember.

When Brian got off the school bus and sat in the middle of the road, saying he would carry me home and his insistence that he wouldn't go home if I didn't get on his back ran through my mind like a picture.

It was the stubbornness that only I knew.

However, everything was now in the past.

'Was I torturing Brian right now for saying I was leaving?'

Was I tormenting Brian thinking, 'Brian, you too must suffer as much as I did,'?
I had no intention of doing that now or ever. Because he was my Brian.
"Okay. I won't leave, Brian."
Thanks to Brian's stubbornness, I shook my head, saying I wouldn't do it like a good child. It was just like Brian and I from a long time ago.
"Anna!"
Brian quickly took off his gloves. It was as if he was taking off his clothes. Then he covered my face with his frozen bare hands. I couldn't tell if Brian's hands were cold or my face was cold. Then he held me in his arms. He tightened his arms around me and rubbed his frozen face against my cheek. Our tears turned to thin ice and turned slippery. Brian's lips slipped on the thin ice of tears and stopped on my lips.
"Brian!"
"Ah, Anna!"
We groaned out each other's names. And I gladly met Brian's lips. As our lips met, I thought, "Now let Brian go, I have to let him go." And I was determined not to leave a guilty conscience in my heart for sending away Brian, who will never be a man to me ever again and who will forever be my younger brother.
I took off my gloves and ran my bare hands over Brian's face. Then I looked into Brian's eyes and said.
"Goodbye, Brian!"
"Goodbye, my love, Anna!"
Weeping, Brian and I hugged each other again. And then we parted.
When I was six years old, I first met a five-year-old Brian and his parents in my Peruvian home. And the following year, we became one family and lived together until now. Brian and I became siblings. But as we grew up, we crossed the boundary drawn by our parents from time to time and looked only at each other with pure hearts. After falling down in front of the boundary, we finally reached the moment when we had to say 'sorry' and 'goodbye'.
I wanted forgiveness from my parents for this farewell ceremony. Because my parents played a part in making sure that Brian and I grew up only knowing each other ever since we were young.
'Goodbye, Brian.'
With these words, the warm wind in my life became freezing cold and disappeared. Then I buried the memories of my first love, that

came with a breeze, deep in my heart.

7. There were rumors

The house was filled with soft and calm music that Brian picked for their unborn baby, the smell of comfort food for Sua's health, and the chatter of Mother and the laughter of Father. It was like Brian and Sua had unpacked a package of bright laughter and happiness that Mother and Father had been waiting for in the quiet house.

After Brian and Father left for work, Mother enjoyed conversing with Sua and I. It was like Mother became a little girl with her daughter and daughter-in-law in front of her.

'I was coming to Canada from England with my parents by boat, I had severe seasickness.'

My mother said she was fifteen years old when she rode on a ship for the first time. The story of how she first met Father, which I had already heard many times, was for Sua. My mother told me the story when she and I were making a quilt for when Brian got married someday.

'I was exhausted from seasickness, when a young man came up to me and offered something, saying, "Try putting this in your mouth." The young man seemed to have noticed my motion sickness. It was a candy with a scent of mint.'

Since this was the first Sua had heard of her Mother's love story, she was looking at Mother with her deep eyes, but I was thinking of another scene. When I was always full of tears from the unfamiliarity, Brian's small hands full of candies and cookies, telling me, 'Share them with me, Anna', I'm sure Brian's warm and kind heart came from Father.

'The scent of mint spread in my mouth, driving away the motion sickness, so I couldn't bite the candy. I kept it in my mouth so the

candy wouldn't melt and disappear.'
Mother squinted her eyes and looked out at the lake beyond the window, where the water began to embrace the fishy smell, as if longing for the moment she received the mint candy.
'I guess that's how a relationship comes. Coming as something trivial but it really isn't and it becomes the most precious thing.... Who would have known that with that one candy, I would get Brian and Anna and we'd live together until I became a grandmother?'
The relationship that came as something trivial but became something most precious.
From the time I first heard those words and still now, I envied my mother. It was because she was looking back on a fulfilling relationship and was happily reminiscing about it now.
'Why didn't Mother, who had such a relationship, not understand Brian and I at the tree house?'
Though my mother said, 'I only knew that you two grew up as siblings', there was a deep sadness in my heart. But it was a feeling that could not be expressed.
Brian could say everything he had in mind, but I couldn't. No matter how much my parents raised me as their daughter and as Brian's older sister, there was a definite line that I couldn't cross and that was my limit. I couldn't just jump into the arms of my parents and say everything acting like a child like Brian. Maybe it wasn't my parents who made me that way, but it was I, myself.
'I was so worried that my son would make me forget my youthful years and just run into a grandmother. But oh, no! This feeling is pretty nice. You probably don't know what I'm talking about. This feeling of having everything. It is the feeling that my soon to be born grandson completes me.'
My mother's expression showed the leisure and satisfaction of a person who truly had it all and enjoyed it to the fullest. How many people in the world could say they were on their way to perfection? With those words, I could guess how happy Mother was with Brian, Sua and the soon to be born baby.
As the sun began to penetrate deeper and deeper into my room, I found myself opening the window often. A gentle breeze blew across Lake Ontario, caressing my face. It was springtime.
Workers who came from Jamaica and Mexico after winter, had

already started working in the vineyards. They tied and pruned the branches that had grown over the past year and became tangled during the winter.

From a distance, they appeared to be standing very quietly wearing only sunshade hats, but their mouths were as busy as their hands. They were probably talking about their family they had left behind, whom they couldn't see until at least the end of October. The young workers who had left their pregnant wives would tell stories of their wives and child, and fathers who had left their young ones would be busy talking about their children.

A young man named Diego was one of the workers from Mexico.
I didn't have a chance to talk with the workers on the farm, but Diego was the exception. On weekends when there wasn't any work at the farm, he would prune the fence, mow the lawn and tend to the garden at our home. Mother and I usually took care of the plants in the garden, but the heavy lifting was left for Diego. My father had been observing Diego's sincerity for several years and entrusted him with housework as well. In particular, after Diego carefully mowed the grass that grew quickly in the sun, the lawn became like a green carpet laid out in the front and back yards.

For several years, Diego had come here from Mexico to work on the farm and at the end of October he would return to his country. He worked hard and spoke very little. When he mowed the lawn or trimmed the fence, it was my job to bring cool drinks on a tray for Diego. Even to me, all Diego did was smile.

'Treat the workers like family members and they'll do everything like their own.'

My mother and father treated him comfortably, so Diego took care of house work as if they were his own. At some point, I had a feeling that Diego was looking at me everytime he passed by.

'How are you, Anna?'
The ever quiet Diego spoke to me that day. It had never happened before, so I stopped and looked at Diego. I got the feeling his dark eyes wanted to say something, but what he said to me was just 'Hello'.

I wondered if Diego might have felt closeness towards me. I was from Peru and Diego was from Mexico. His skin tone, dark hair, and facial features were similar to mine. And the biggest common thingDiego and I had was that we were both living away from home.

'Oh, Diego, how is your mother's health?'
Diego, who would always respond with a smile when I handed him a drink, was talking to me for the first time so I just asked how his mother was doing. Mother told me last year that before Diego left for Mexico, he had come to say goodbye to my mother and told her about his ailing mother and how he needed to stay by her side all winter long.
Tears suddenly welled up and Diego bit his lips. He looked like he was suppressing something inside. Then he said, 'My mother passed away'.
'Oh, I'm so sorry!'
I felt guilty for unintentionally asking for his mother's well-being.
'My mother died when I was by her side...
I think Diego was trying to say that he was lucky he was by his mother's side when she passed. I didn't know what to say to comfort Diego anymore. Just talking to Diego was unexpected.
'Thank you for asking Anna.'
Diego's black eyes filled with tears were reminded of my older brother Mario. My older brother Mario also spoke very little and was very thoughtful. Even if my brother Mario did not speak loud, there were times when I could read his mind just by looking at his eyes. Diego too, who was as reserved as Mario, was a person who knew when to speak out when he needed to.
As I entered the house, I felt Diego looking at my back.
Because it was Sunday, and there wasn't any farm work, Diego was driving the lawn mower in the yards. As the days warmed up, the grass grew more vigorously, so Diego worked on the lawn on weekends when he wasn't working on the farm.
My mother and Sua had gone to buy baby supplies and Father and Brian were at the winery.
'Anna, I'm sorry we're going just by ourselves. Let's go together next time.'
My mother didn't forget to apologize so I wouldn't feel left out. After Mother and Sua left, I had the house to myself so I opened a book that I borrowed from the local library.
The sound of the lawnmower broke the quiet Sunday afternoon. On days like today, the thunderous sound of the lawnmower seemed like it could cause waves on the calm lake. After finishing the front yard, Diego went out to the back yard to mow the lawn, overlooking the lake

with his ears covered. He might've been listening to music. The grass had stopped growing during the winter and turned green in the spring sunlight. When it was cut off by the machine Diego was driving, it smelled of strong grass. The smell of the fishy water from the lake and the smell of grass blended together into the scent of spring.

I closed the book I was reading and prepared a drink. Today, I was doing my mother's job, which was to bring drinks to Diego when he was working. I looked at Diego holding my drink tray, then looked at the lake while waiting for Diego to finish mowing the lawn. The windless Lake Ontario was like a cloudless sky.

For me, Lake Ontario is Peru's Lake Titicaca. The highest celestial lake in South America formed by the melting waters of the Andean snow mountains.

My real father had caught and sold turchas on Lake Titicaca. My mother cooked with the leftovers and Mario sometimes said he wished father didn't sell all of the fish every day. I used to agree with him saying, 'Me too'.

After I became family with Brian, me and Brian went fishing together with Father. My father would go to Lake Erie, about an hour away from home, or fished in the nearby Niagara River. Father caught any number of small fish, mainly perch, in Lake Erie, but it was illegal to catch more than the set number of bass or sunfish. When father caught a fish, he released it back into the water. Father just enjoyed fishing with Brian and I.

'When I was young, my father and Uncle liked to take me fishing. Adults had to have a license and each person could catch six black bass or something like that. I was young back then so I could catch six fish without a license. They took me along to catch six more for my share, but I didn't catch any.'

When my father released the fish he caught and told us about his childhood, I thought of my Peruvian father, who sold turcha that he caught in Lake Titicaca and my mother who cooked the leftovers.

When Lake Ontario reminded me of Lake Titicaca, it brought back old and faded memories of my real mother, father, and my real brother Mario. The zamponya was the only thing that kept the memories of my childhood from fading.

Today, Lake Ontario was as quiet as a cloudless sky and only the noise of the lawnmower that Diego drove disturbed the calm Sunday

afternoon.
"Anna!"
I had forgotten that Diego was looking at me as I looked out at the lake thinking of my family in Titicaca.
"Anna, have you been waiting for me?"
Diego hung his earplugs around his neck.
"Diego, are you done?"
As I handed him the drink, Diego grinned.
'Thank you, Anna'
He grabbed the cup and gulped it down.
"Thank you, Diego, for always taking care of the lawn."
I said while waiting for Diego to finish the drink. I was more comfortable talking to Diego since we spoke last time.
"You're welcome. I do it because I want to."
Diego smiled again. I was thinking that Diego might not be a shy person, since he talked a little bit more and laughed a lot more.
"What are you doing here, Anna?
Then the door to the cellar facing the lake opened and Brian, who was supposed to be at the winery, came out.
"What are you doing here, Brian?"
I looked at Brian surprised, because Brian didn't like going down to the basement after his traumatic experience, even as an adult.
"I came to find something to eat."
Brian knew that Mother and Sua had gone shopping and maybe thought that I would be home alone.
"Hey, Diego!"
Brian's expression wasn't so bright as he greeted Diego.
"Do you need to talk to Anna?"
Brian's rather straightforward words sounded harsh to me. Brian's tone seemed to be asking, "Diego, what are you doing? Why are you talking to Anna with a smile?" I looked at Diego for a moment. I thought that Diego must have felt the same way and I felt sorry for making him feel embarrassed.
"Yes, I have something to tell Anna."
But then Diego said something I wasn't expecting. I looked at both Diego and Brian. Diego was relaxed and Brian seemed to have gotten a little peeved. I was at a loss between these two men and why Diego said something that was not true. If Diego answered 'no' there wouldn't

have been any problem, but he put me in an awkward position.
"Oh? Why don't you tell me what you have to say to Anna?"
Brian quickly took on the role of the boss. More like the master speaking to the servant. Why did Brian's tone make me think of Michael when I was young? I shook my head the moment I saw the image of Michael, who teased me as a child, in Brian's tone and attitude. Because it meant discrimination and ignorance.
"Why do I have to tell you what I want to say to Anna?"
But Diego was very different from me when I was a girl who was teased and didn't say anything. Diego set his eyes on Brian and asked 'why?' with an insincere attitude.
The atmosphere suddenly took an unexpected turn when Brian appeared and I didn't know what to do. I wanted to sit down, cover my face, and hide, just like when I was a child. But it couldn't. I was no longer the Anna of old and this situation was definitely because of me.
"What do you mean? You mean you have something private to say to Anna?"
"Private or public, it is not for you to meddle. Can you excuse us, Brian? I haven't finished talking to Anna yet."
Brian wanted to take down Diego and Diego responded by ignoring it.
"Don't you know Anna was my sister, Diego?"
"Stop it, Brian!"
I restrained Brian rather than Diego. It was childish to me to see two grown men arguing. Diego, who I always thought was a quiet person, was no different.
Brian, who suddenly came out and started meddling, was getting red with his emotions rising. In my eyes, Brian seemed to have lost his composure because he was driven into a corner by Diego's rebellious replies.
"Oh, Anna was your older sister, Brian? But what about the rumors?"
Diego had said something unnecessary. A rumor. A rumor about Brian and I. A rumor about me and Brian that Diego knew which Brian and I didn't. What was it? Moreover, if Diego had heard it, the rumor would have been well-known among the farm workers.
'That was the reason Diego was looking at me that day!'
The realization of Diego's gaze on my back since that day was because of 'that rumor' hit me right on the forehead.
Brian and I looked at Diego at the same time and this time Diego bit

his lip, as if regretting what he had said, then shut his eyes tightly and bowed his head. I was thinking that Diego was more imprudent than I thought.

"A rumor?"

Brian asked sharply.

Diego, who seemed to be in a corner, suddenly raised his head.

"People say, 'You two are in love. That's what the people who were with you at the winter grape harvest last winter said. Rumors, of course, but you should be more careful of your older sister, Brian."

Diego must've thought the water was already spilt, so he told Brian about the rumor.

As I was listening to Diego's completely unexpected words, I felt dizzy. So, that day, on the farm in the early morning when the snow was piled up, the workers who witnessed our parting spread the word and it reached Diego's ears.

The midwinter grape harvest was done by resident workers, who did not have to return to their country. So, according to Diego, the scene of two head-lamps illuminating each other was floating around among the workers and Diego, who often came to take care of our house, was taking the rumor seriously. But, because Brian tried to interfere in the conversation between his older sister and a worker, Diego had suddenly told us the rumor.

"What do the workers know... And you should be careful with what you say!"

Brian was surprised by Diego's unexpected words and tried to find his composure by scolding him.

"I admit it. I was out of line. But you should be careful too, because there are a lot of eyes around here."

Diego casually accepted his fault and looked at Brian again. Diego's sincerity was contained in his eyes. If Brian hadn't appeared, if Brian hadn't argued first, then at least those words wouldn't have come out of Diego's mouth.

"Diego, who do you think you are?"

It was only then that Brian asked out-right. He must've thought that Diego was not an easy person to deal with by the way he spoke.

"Me? As you know, I am a worker on your farm. It will end this year, though."

"What does that mean?"

Brian and I looked at Diego, who was trusted by my father, when he said he would be out at the end of this year. Only then did Diego chuckle and said,

"I have to go back to my regular job. This year is the last. I also wanted to thank Tom and his wife, and also to Ms. Anna. They're the ones who welcomed me. I just wanted to say my sincere thanks to Anna. Actually, I didn't even have time to say that, face to face like this."

After Diego spoke Brian seemed to have softened a bit and asked again.

'Farming isn't your main job?'

"It's the experience I need for my full-time job. I'll tell you before I leave for Mexico this fall. Now I have more lawn to mow, so excuse me."

Then he covered his ears again and started the lawnmower. Brian and I, looking at Diego, came back to the house through the basement door. I thought he was a mysterious character and Brian didn't say anything just like he agreed with my thinking.

"I see Diego was here."

Returning from the farm, my father saw the neatly trimmed garden and knew that Diego had stopped by. When Brian answered 'yes', I was afraid that the rumors of what Diego told us would come out of my father's mouth.

"Whatever he does, he is a faithful young man."

My father's trust in Diego was very deep. It was because Diego took good care of everything as if they were his own business.

"You trust Diego too much."

Brian said, listening quietly. Perhaps because of what happened during the day, it sounded like dissatisfaction to my ears because my father trusted Diego too much.

"It's been several years since I knew Diego, but the young man hasn't changed."

Brian was well aware of how sincere and faithful Diego was and how much mother and father trusted him. But Diego's tough attitude during the day seemed to make Brian uncomfortable.

"It is a great blessing to meet someone faithful in life, Brian."

I had no idea how persuasive my father's words would be for Brian, who didn't like Diego. Anyway, it was fortunate that the rumor that Brian and I would've never known had it not been for Diego, had not reached my father's ears.

That rumor, the farewell parting at dawn in the middle of winter,

when Brian and I held each other at the grape harvest, must have been quite interesting to the workers because they knew us as siblings.
Just as I took care every day to get rid of all the crumbs of emotions that remained in my heart even after painfully cutting out my bitter love, I only hoped from the bottom of my heart that the workers on our farm also disregarded the stories they had seen and heard like the winds of the time.

8. Swayed by Chattering

I still wanted to call it spring, but summer was like a rude occupational force, pushing back spring and treading on the ground. As if saying if there ever was a long winter, if there ever was snow covering the ankles, the impatient summer mobilized heat to urge things to blossom again.

The grass was exceptionally weak against the heat. The green grass in the snow was sensitive to summer heat. After a few days, the grass turned yellow and dried up, but soon returned to green thanks to streaks of rain showers.

One of the first sounds to signal the departure of winter was the noise of the lawn mower. When the grass had stopped growing in the cold, it grew into a messy shape in the sunlight and those who had been lazy during the winter must start with the lawn mower. When your neighbor's lawn is as clean as the hair of a child who got a long-delayed bath and haircut one day, you can't just stand by and watch. In order to not be labeled lazy, you needed to mow the lawn once a week to keep the yard neat and tidy.

When the weather warms up, lawn mowers are more arrogant than the midday sun, screaming loudly from the early morning to escape the midday heat.

Even if the quiet neighborhood suffered from noise every day, no one blamed anyone, so they had no choice but to say, "Oh, we must mow the lawn too."

Like grass that grows even after being mowed, fruit trees bearing fruit in places where spring flowers have fallen, are quietly busy extracting juice in the sunlight. People walk or ride bicycles under the blazing sunlight without fear.

At sunset, three or four people gather to grill meat and drink wine, so

the long and deep winter is just a forgotten season for people.
When the land was plagued by the noise of the lawn mower, Lake Ontario was swayed by the sound of ships of all kinds. After a cold and gloomy winter, the lake might have longed for the noise of the ships. All sounds must have been the sounds the lake had been waiting during the winter, from the sound of the motors of a plump boat going fishing through the early morning mist, to the sound of the laughter of people holding wine glasses on sailboats enjoying themselves from day to sunset while elegantly raising their triangular sails.
Rather than being a lake by itself, a lake is only completed when it harmonizes with the fish, the waterfowl, people's vehicles, and the color of the sky overlooking it. People enjoy to their heart's content in the bosom of the overflowing lake and enjoy festivals.
A town with a lake, fruits, and wine. For the locals, summer was a season of exciting festivals.
As summer entered, the workers pruned the fully grown leaves on the chest of the vines and clusters of grapes drooping like the breasts of a mother. Now that the leaves were removed, the breasts that had been hiding would be able to soak up the sunlight to their heart's content. Most of those ripe grapes turn into wine, but some were served as table grapes, as fruits.
'If there is no big change in the weather, I think it will be a bountiful harvest. Very plump and good'
My father loved to walk slowly along the furrows on the farm and watch the grapes grow.
Father's personality was optimistic. When it snowed a lot, he liked that the vidal grapes had a sweet taste, and when it rained, he liked the water needed for fruit trees. When the summer drought was long, he relaxed, saying, 'What are you worrying about when the sea-like Lake Ontario is in front of you?'
Also, when the wind blew, he said, 'The vines bind themselves together and become stronger'.
My father viewed all seasons and all phenomena positively in connection with farming. That's why my father's farm and winery seemed to be thriving more.
'Our daughter-in-law, Sua, is about to give birth, and we have to harvest our first grapes. We're going to be very busy.'
As Sua's childbirth date neared, mother's heart seemed to be busy as

well.

Mother washed and dried the diapers that she had already made. She also prepared the baby jacket and blanket. She could easily buy paper diapers at the local mart, but mother bought cloth and made diapers from them herself. She was the one who was looking for work and she was very happy with it.

With a more relaxed mind, I could look at Sua's full stomach and face Brian again. It was probably because I had released all the torture-like daily things at the dawn, that I had to comprehend, spoke and laughed as if nothing happened while embracing them deep inside me.

When I woke up, I prepared coffee first and then had breakfast with my mother.

Mother was always upset when Brian finished his breakfast with only coffee and toast. Mother said he wasn't getting the nutrition when he ate breakfast like that and put milk, fried eggs and bacon on toast, along with the fruit. She sometimes made porridge with oatmeal, topped it with milk and brown sugar, and added blueberries for breakfast. It was a simple breakfast meal.

'I think my mom still thinks I need to grow taller.'

Drinking milk reluctantly at mother's request, Brian used to complain like a child. Their conversation always ended with Brian accepting Mother's words. After coming from Korea, Brian seemed to laugh more and show affection, especially to Mother. The peace of everyday life with friendly conversations and laughter filled the house like the midsummer sunlight.

"Can Anna come with me to today's meeting?"

At the breakfast table mother looked at me and asked. When mother went out, she always drove a car by herself, but sometimes I drove and accompanied Mother from time to time. It was a gathering of wives, so it wouldn't be fun, but I gladly followed my mother.

When I joined the meeting while driving, I had access to trivial information about the everyday world over my shoulder, such as volunteer work at the women's group. I also learned that the information the wives exchanged among them directly or indirectly affected the husbands' winery operations.

In their conversation, there was jealousy without knowing it, and there was comparison and competition. Nevertheless, there was dignity and an exclusive line drawn in its own way. Husbands in the same business were practically engaged and wives were engaged in the business through dialogue among themselves. Husbands were forced to listen to what their wives were saying. So in the end, wives also indirectly participated in the business. In that sense, the regular meetings of the wives were important to each of them.

My mother, with her make-up meticulously done and wearing a light blue dress that slightly covered her shoulders, was not like any other housewife doing the housekeeping and caring for the plants in the garden. Every time she went to a meeting once a month, my mother was an elegant lady.

The place I drove to was the Golf Club Restaurant.

Lake Ontario, the largest lake in the Great Lakes located inland in North America, meets Lake Huron and Michigan, and then joins Lake Erie, and flows back into the Niagara River, then plummets at Niagara Falls and is swayed through a gorge. It is the place where the water can relax and enjoy after a long journey.

At the end of the Niagara River and the beginning of Lake Ontario, seen from the window of the car, a sailboat with its sails was being pushed by the wind.

"Joanne, you came with your daughter today!"

If other wives' daughters or daughters-in-law joined together to drive their mothers, we would sit around and talk separately, but today I was alone, so I sat among the wives.

"You're going to be a grandmother soon, Joanne!"

The wives congratulated my mother in unison.

"But your daughter-in-law is South or North?"

The wives asked questions about Korea.

"Of course South Korea."

"Joanne must be happy with such a pretty and courteous daughter and a daughter-in-law..."

"Thanks. Actually, I was planning to come with my daughter-in-law today and to introduce her to you, but she's close to birth, so I told her to rest at home."

Actually, my mother would not want to make her daughter-in-law awkward in front of many wives, as it was clear that the daughter-in-law, who got married without a wedding, was in the middle of some rumors that were probably on the lips of many people for a while.

But in fact, it was something that even my mother did not understand.

When Brian said he was getting married in Korea, he told his parents not to come, who were preparing to go to the wedding with great anticipation, and said he would tell them the reason when he returned home to Canada, but he still hadn't said anything.

'What story was there between the two, so why were the two exchanging rings without a wedding? I really feel like I lost my son, Anna.'

My parents, who were planning to have a grand wedding for their only son, were greatly disappointed when they had to cancel their trip to Korea.

So, even though my mother wanted to introduce Sua at the wives' meeting, she brought me along using Sua's heavy body as an excuse.

"Okay, your daughter-in-law should take care of herself."

"I envy you, Joanne. Our second child also needs to marry. Is there no good bride?"

When the conversation began with a child, Mrs. Evans looked at the wives in attendance. Mrs. Evans had publicly asked all wives to play matchmaker for her own child. Since all of them are wives with over-aged children, the marriage of their children was also a topic of conversation with interest.

"You mean Michael?"

The name Michael, which came out of someone's mouth, seemed to hit my heart as I was sitting there involuntarily. I put down my cup of coffee and looked out the window to the lake to calm my beating heart. The sail boat had already been blown away by the wind and a speedboat with its head raised was running through the water.

This symptom of mine, the sinking feeling from the heart just by hearing the name 'Michael', must be due to the memories that were deeply engraved in me even after all these years.

"Oh, does Anna know Michael?"

Suddenly, Mrs. Gilmour spoke to me. At Mrs. Gilmore's question, all the women's eyes fell on me, and I was tense again.

Michael Evans, how could I not know him?

He was the child who hurt me so badly when I was young. He was the bully I was afraid to meet by chance in the same neighborhood. I already knew that Michael was the second son of Mrs. Evans, but Mrs. Gilmore's question was so unexpected that I, sitting among the wives, was very upset.

“Yeah, Anna knows Michael well. My Anna and Brian studied with Michael.”
My mother, who had guessed how I felt, responded swiftly instead of me. Although it may seem ordinary, none of the wives could have even guessed that there were spikes in my mother's words. It must have been a spike of emotion for how much her children suffered because of that Michael.
“Did Michael and Anna know each other well? Good for you! By the way, Michael and Anna, what do you think?”
Mrs. Gilmore arbitrarily interpreted that Michael and I were already well acquainted, and then abruptly dragged me in, saying it was just a conversation.

I just wanted to get up on the spot and get out of this absurd situation that suddenly happened. At Mrs. Gilmore's words, my mother and the other wives were silent for a brief moment, as if muted. My mother and Mrs. Evans looked at Mrs. Gilmore with their eyes wide open then my mother and Mrs. Evans looked at each other. Sitting there, I was an invisible person.
“Two young people know each other well and both families can trust each other, don’t they?”
The words of Mrs. Gilmore were verbose, as if she was going to push through to the end because she had just come up with it anyway. Even my mother, who had already spoken sharply, was looking at me without saying anything. My mother seemed to be embarrassed.
“Actually, Michael had an ordeal.”
At that time, Mrs. Evans mentioned something that everyone already knew roughly, but kept her mouth shut, as if confessing that it was an ordeal.
Everyone's eyes turned to Mrs. Evans at once. It was because Mrs. Evans directly mentioned Michael's ordeal, which everyone knew, at a time when the marriage proposal wasn’t even thought of. The wives all kept their mouths shut, watching what came out of Mrs. Evans' mouth. It was supposed to be a confession of Michael's alcohol treatment that everyone knew but kept silent.

“It’s all in the past. Michael works hard and we all know how good Anna is.”
Mrs. Gilmore stepped in again and reassured Mrs. Evans and my

mother, who was suddenly surprised and bewildered, by clearing up all of Michael's past experiences and by complimenting me a bit. Mrs. Evans said no further about her son's ordeal.

"Young people these days have clear ideas about themselves..."

My mother, who seemed to have a lot to say, mumbled her words, suffocating the completely unexpected atmosphere. I thought that my mother, who knew me well, was not able to cut Mrs. Gilmore's words because she was in front of the local wives.

"We're just trying to connect two young people. Young people these days are smart."

But, Mrs. Gilmore was tenacious. It was as if Michael and I were the subject of today's meeting.

"If two families become one family with children, there will be no wineries in this area to compare."

When Mrs. Ford, who had been quietly listening to the conversation, joked, Mrs. Evans said, "You're going too far, Mrs. Ford". My mother was also in shock and had a shaky expression on her face, neither smiling nor angry.

Today's conversation of elegant, educated wives was disappointing, at least to me. They were rude, all of them intervening in other people's very private affairs, and moreover, putting me on the spot. I regretted going to the meeting with my mother.

Whenever my mother wanted to take me to a meeting, I joined because she asked me to. My mother liked it when I came with her, so I gladly joined the meeting, even if it was uncomfortable for me. It wouldn't have anything to do with my habit of answering 'yes' rather than 'no'. But today, I should have said 'no', but it was too late to regret it.

I wanted to get up, but I couldn't go out alone, so I had no choice but to sit there, eating and drinking tea, and waiting for the wives to relax and finish their conversation.

On the way home, my mother was silent. It must have been because of what Mrs. Gilmore had said. Even my mother knew a little bit about what Michael was like to me, if not as much as Brian did.

Michael, how could I forget that name?

When I first came to Canada and went to school with Brian, he was the first and the most persistent child who followed me and bullied me.

'Why are you different from Brian?'
'Go to your home, Anna.'
'Anna is dumb!'
As Michael tumbled around me and annoyed me, I squatted over my face without saying a word. Whenever that happened, Brian, who came out from nowhere, would clench his fists and stare at Michael.
'Brian, why are you different from Anna?'
'Why are you on Anna's side?'
Michael's bully behavior never stopped and even when Brian talked to our parents, they weren't too involved. Michael was the son of one of my father's friends that my parents knew all too well, and my parents must have thought that adults shouldn't be involved in children's affairs. But the wives who knew nothing about Michael and me were trying to tie me with Michael. It was a very uncomfortable place, but I couldn't show any signs of it.
"Now the meeting is tiring."
Said my mother, who was silent until we got home. It was a meeting where there would always have been invisible competition among wives, but today it was clear that the topic of marriage added to the competition, which made my mother more tired.
"My daughter must also meet a good young man, but I have nothing to say to you, Anna."
I was thinking about other things without answering my mother. It was about Michael, when Mrs. Evans stopped talking after Mrs Gilmore intercepted her. Because it is a small town, rumors quickly swelled and spread.
According to the rumors, Michael was being treated for alcoholism and that after a while Michael would finish treatment and work at his father's winery.
Even though we lived in the same neighborhood, we never saw each other. He was someone I didn't want to meet by chance.

"When I welcomed you into my family, I made a promise to your real father and brother that I would raise you as my daughter."
It was clear that my mother was either shocked or exhausted by the words exchanged among the wives at the gathering. It's because she said something she had never said before. That was why I had to be my mother's daughter.
At that time, as I remember, my brother Mario was begging my real

father not to let me go. He said at first and then yelled, saying, "You shouldn't let her go."

'If only your mother is here now, I won't let Mamani go, Mario. They said they will raise our Mamani as their own daughter, didn't they?' My father scolded my brother while trying to comfort him and then a loud noise broke out between the two of them. When my real father got drunk on chicha, my brother drank too. I hated seeing my father and brother quarrel over me.

"You are an overly good daughter to me, Anna. Above all, you are the older sister who influenced Brian to grow into a bright person. You have done everything your mother and father would do for Brian."

I could feel that my mother's words were sincere. And I knew how much my mother loved me. But why did my mother put such a crude boundary between Brian and me? No matter how we started as older sister and younger brother, it was too harsh of a boundary for me.

The boundary that my mother drew between Brian and I, when we were growing in body and mind, made me realize that there are borders in everything I do.

The boundaries I felt while growing up may have acted as a factor for me to distance myself from my mother above all else and to treat my mother in a difficult way.

For something that Brian would not have hesitated to do, I was conscious of politeness before speaking or acting and that was the limit I made. Since that line was inside me, I would have answered 'yes' even if I wanted to say 'no without being ready to express my thoughts. It was something I couldn't overcome even if Brian and I grew up as siblings in the same family.

"How was today's meeting? Did Anna go too?"

At the dinner table, my father casually asked about my mother's daily routine. My father would have asked if there was any new information about the business my mother might have heard of at the wives' gatherings.

"Oh, well, Mrs. Gilmore brought up the matchmaking between Michael and Anna."

It was natural for my mother to talk about the meeting as part of her daily routine, so I just listened.

"You mean Michael, Paul's second son?"

As if unexpectedly, my father looked at my mother and said,

"Not Michael, no!"
It was then, just like the young Brian in his childhood who suddenly appeared from somewhere and yelled at Michael who was making fun of me when we were kids, that Brian shouted. Everyone in the family looked at Brian in surprise. Sua looked at Brian first and I was biting my lips with my eyes closed.
"Mrs. Gilmore said those are all things of the past."
Mother was momentarily taken aback by Brian's unexpected reaction and my mother told us what Mrs. Gilmore said. It was about the ordeal that Michael had to go through.
"Not Michael!"
Brian was stubborn.
"Yeah, Michael didn't leave very good memories for Anna."
My father also responded to what Brian said.
"Michael, I know. As for Anna, Michael doesn't deserve it!"
Brian was adamant. I looked up at Brian, raising my lowered eyes. It was because Brian was telling our family what I wanted to say in front of the wives on my behalf.
"And quitting alcohol is not easy. You never know when he'll touch it again."
That was also correct. How can he easily cut off the drinking habit, which he had gradually taken up for a long time? It was a thought that popped up in my mind when Mrs. Gilmore spoke during the day. So Brian raised his voice for me, explaining why Michael and I shouldn't be involved.

However, it was very inconvenient for me to watch this situation while Brian was saying what I wanted to say. Both mother and father were dumbfounded and looked at Brian with their mouths closed. Sua was staring at Brian blankly as if she was mesmerized. As if I was already deeply entangled with Michael, as if I was standing naked in front of my family and listening to his blames, I was so embarrassed.

This was exactly about me, but I couldn't understand why Brian was so sensitive or why he came forward when I kept my mouth shut even when the words I wanted to say came all the way up to my throat. Moreover, it was in front of Sua.
Brian's behavior was like that of Mrs. Gilmore, who tried to entangle me with Michael without even realizing I was in front of her.

“Brian makes sense. Alcohol is everywhere and it won't be easy for Michael to quit."
When my father finally took Brian's side, my mother couldn't speak any more and put on a perplexed expression on her face. Her expression was like an orphan with no place to depend on. In this unfair situation, the resentment hidden within me suddenly lifted its head.
To Brian, who came out in front of Diego and still now, took the first step in my affairs, I was even more antipathetic, saying, 'I know that much.'

"I will see him"
Finally I went forward. I wanted to cut off that presumptuous involvement of Brian. It shouldn't have been so hard to push Mother who wanted to share her daily routine with the family.
Suddenly the atmosphere froze.
“Anna!”
My mother and father looked at me with their eyes wide open and Brian yelled at me.
“It was when we were kids.”
When I, who had always listened quietly, spoke up against Brian, my father and mother, Sua and Brian, all shut their mouths.
“Anna, you don’t care what you heard during the meeting,"
In a situation where my mother hadn't politely received marriage proposals from Mrs. Evans and in a situation where Brian is now protesting, my mother tried to restrain me by denigrating the conversation at this afternoon's meeting as chattering.
“If I have a chance, Mother.”
But I also did not break my stubbornness. I was no different from Brian.
“Anna, no! You know what kind of person Michael is.”
Brian was still worked up.
“I'll take care of it, Brian.”
Everyone was bewildered at my unobtrusive and unconventional appearance. Maybe Brian remembered my words, 'I'm leaving,' and thought I was just throwing myself at Michael without a second thought. It was Brian who knew me the most.
“But it’s not Michael!”
Brian didn't give up either.

Sua had been quietly listening to the conversation, got up and went upstairs. It seemed like a rejection of Brian's pretest.

"Okay, let's reconsider this, because there's nothing concrete about it."

Suddenly, the atmosphere became awkward with the incident, and father stepped in.

"How could there be such a commotion in our house because of Mrs. Gilmore..."

My mother resented Mrs. Gilmore for bringing it up first. My mother couldn't stand the fact that her son and daughter had created a confrontation in a house where peace was as full as summer sunshine, in a house full of friendly conversation and laughter.

In fact, the conversations of the wives were uncomfortable for me there, but those were words that could be shared by any parent with an over-aged child.

"You should have said 'no' on the spot, Mom!"

But Brian shot an arrow of resentment at mother again. It was resentment against mother for not actively blocking Mrs. Gilmore's words. It was also his resentment against mother that your daughter was harassed by Michael when she was young and why mother would let her hear it again.

Mother, who heard the complaints from her son again, looked blankly at Brian.

"Brian, you are being too sensitive."

This time, instead of mother, father stepped in and scolded Brian.

"I thought this was over. But you're going too far with what Anna wants, Brian."

Finally, mother revealed her sadness.

"Then why did Mom pretend not to know Anna's feelings?"

"That time," Brian said to Mother again.

"That time?"

Father and mother both opened their eyes wide to Brian at the same time.

"You said 'no' that time, didn't you?"

"Stop it, Brian!"

This time I put the brakes on Brian's words. At their son's rather aggressive remarks, father straightened his face and mother shut her mouth.

I couldn't understand Brian's attitude towards tormenting mother by bringing up the past with me as an excuse. It was as if he thought he was free to show his temper in front of mother.

"All the past, Brian..."

It was only then that Mother seemed to remember the thing in the tree house.

I couldn't be there, so I went to the kitchen. In the end, things escalated because of me.

"It's Anna's life."

Brian again lashed out at his mother.

"I only knew that."

My mother barely said

I couldn't understand my mother, who couldn't raise her voice in front of Brian.

"I was trying to keep my promise to her Peruvian family, that I would raise her as my daughter, and I thought it was to protect Anna's happiness."

As if mother had just made up her mind, she revealed things from a long time ago to Brian. So mother was saying that she did everything she could to keep her promise to my real father in Peru.

"You don't know how much Anna suffered because of Michael. Anna was terribly afraid that she might run into Michael by accident on the way. What I'm really worried about is how Anna might throw herself at Michael..."

Brian bit his tongue, unable to finish his words. Then he stood still and went upstairs. Only father and mother were sitting there.

'As if tossing herself to Michael...'

Brian's words pierced my marrow. Only Brian, who knew how I felt, could say that.

Michael was the kid who teased me the most because of the color and appearance of my skin since I first went to school. Brian was right when he said that Michael was the kid who teased mr the most.

'If you meet Michael on the way, don't be afraid, Anna. I'm with you.'

I trusted Brian. Brian knew better than anyone because he was there whenever I was teased by Michael.

There were also rumors that Michael was being treated for alcohol when he became a young man. There was a time when I wondered what caused the son of a carefree wealthy family to become addicted to alcohol at such an early age.

My real father in Peru and my brother Mario, who didn't accept the fact that I was adopted, also liked to drink, so I thought maybe Michael wasn't a bad guy.

My real father and my brother didn't drink because they were bad people. They probably drank only because they couldn't find any other way to resolve their grievances and dissatisfaction and because alcohol was always readily available.

I thought it might be because there was something cramped inside Michael that he wanted to unravel, so he might have depended on the wine that was always nearby. Fortunately, even though we lived in the same neighborhood, we had never met by chance, so that was all I was interested in Michael.

I got out of the kitchen and went to my parents. My mother, who had been sad and embarrassed by her child after telling him what happened during the day at the meeting, quietly closed her eyes. My father sat silently.

"I'm sorry, father, mother."

I apologized for raising my voice with Brian in front of my parents. I was even more apologetic for having troubled my mother.

The aggression in front of his parents was already excessive with just Brian. My parents were also people who suffered physically and mentally with their children. Knowing all the feelings of my parents, I shouldn't have done that.

"Did you really mean it? To meet Michael that way, Anna?"

Sure enough, my mother looked at me. My mother's face was like a low hanging cloud.

"Mother!"

What could I say?

Knowing all the circumstances, I was swayed by the emotions that arose within me, and I spilled it because I couldn't control it, so it was my responsibility.

"Anna, we neglected to look after you."

My father, who spared words in everything, spoke.

"My daughter, I thought that if we laughed together like we used to, we would laugh and live together."

This time my mother opened her arms and hugged me.

'If we laugh together, we will live with a smile..'

It was only from that smile that I knew that it was torture. It was natural that parents who had never experienced such a thing did not know. It was natural that parents who were in the bliss of waiting for their children, daughter-in-law, and grandchildren to be born after a long time did not know.

"Not all people know that they are getting older, Anna."

"That's right, there are times when we don't even know how Anna feels."

I was rather embarrassed by my parents' candid statements that was like a confession.

It was a day of unexpected regrets. Even when I went to bed, I couldn't get a good night's sleep. I was very dissatisfied with myself for arguing with Brian in front of my parents.

9. Diego Leaves

After eight hours of labor, Sua finally gave birth to a baby boy. It had been a while since the cry of a baby rang throughout the house and Father laughed all day long while Mother, as if she had never raised a baby, said, 'I think Ian is hungry.' Mother seemed to have forgotten that babies could cry even when their diapers were wet. Even if the baby was really hungry and crying, Sua with her swollen breast couldn't help but move slowly, so it was Brian who was busy, not knowing what to do.

'It's not easy being a father.'

When our eyes met, Brian gave me a sheepish smile.

I was anxious to carry Ian, Brian's first baby, who was still eating and sleeping. In my hometown of Peru, mothers carried their babies on their backs. Though I can't remember, I must have grown up on my mother's back.

It was a summer full of sunshine and when the right amount of rain fell, a new life was born in the house.

With the help of diligent workers and with the weather good, the grapes were ripening and in the meantime, the grapes for the table were also harvested.

The crop was good and the owners and workers of each farm were satisfied. My father, who had his first grandson, invited the workers to share food and invited musicians to accompany music with wine. It was wine made from grapes grown and harvested by the workers' hands. The excited people got up and danced. In my eyes, they were wonderful people who worked hard, ate, drank and danced to music. Diego was among them too.

Last time Diego suddenly had an argument with Brian, he said this would be the last year of working on the farm. When I saw him dancing, I suddenly remembered what he said. That meant that if Diego returned home this time, he would never come back and he would not be able to manage our house. I was just getting to know people, but I was already sad that I would never see Diego smiling and talking in the crowd again.

By mid-October, the workers were preparing to return to Jamaica or Mexico and they would return in February or March of next year, towards the end of winter. In winter when they are not here, the workers who lived here took care of the winter plants and harvested grapes for ice wine in the surrounding green houses.
As the temperature dropped, the grass stopped growing, so you couldn't even hear the lawn mower in the neighborhood. Today was Diego's last mowing of the year at our house.
While I was looking out the window, Diego was putting more effort into cleaning every nook and cranny because today was the last day he was mowing the lawn at my house. I climbed the tree house while Diego was mowing the lawn. For a long winter, the tree house will hibernate deep in the bosom of an old oak tree, as no one will come to visit. Tree house will look forward to seeing us again in the spring with the zamponya melody I played and the countless conversations Brian and I left behind.

For me, the tree house was a treasure chest filled with colorful memories that I sometimes want to secretly open and look inside. When I open the box, there are water birds flying over the deep blue Titicaca Lake, my mother who died early, my father who caught turcha at sunset, and my brother Mario who played the zamponya. One day, in the box, there was Brian who read a book on my lap while I was knitting. And I, while knitting, was sweeping up the hair that covered Brian's forehead.
There's also Brian and I climbing the tree leaving the ladder behind, a tray of cookies my mother baked, Brian, who pretended not to be but touched me with his long, white hands, Brian who already had voice changes, Brian, who was suffering from nightmares and confided in the memories of the kidnapping, and my clumsy moments of comfort, and Brian, oh, my Brian, who was still holding me behind my back while I was playing the zamponya.

Looking back on the memories with Brian in the treasure box, that was the last time. My mother fell off the ladder and when she emphasized the boundary with the clear word of 'sibling', I could not reject my mother's words, so Brian left for Korea. It was the last time I remembered the hand that was still wrapped around my shoulder, Brian's breath buried in the nape of my neck, and even his heartbeat.

My treasure chest, called the tree house, awakens not only sight but also hearing. These are the sounds of my pre-adoption life and post-adoption life that I vaguely remember when I was seven years old.

When I open the box, Lake Titicaca spreads out in front of my eyes and I hear my real mother's voice calling out to me, 'My pretty Mamani!'. I hear my real father's voice calling to me: 'Mamani, see these fish.' when he caught turcha and returned home happily,

I even heard the voice of my older brother Mario, who was playing the zamponya, saying, 'You have to put a tube on the tip of your lower lip and breathe out through the tube, just like when you blow out the air on the tip of your tongue.'

After my brother finished playing, he said to me, 'Seven tenths of my breath is blown away and the remaining three are hitting the tube and making a sound. It's the sound of longing that calls out the sound of the flying seven-half.'

I thought the zamponya is a solitary instrument that sings the rustling of the wind in the reeds of Lake Titicaca and sometimes evokes nostalgia.

The place where I played the zamponya, longing for Peru, the place where Brian and I spent the most time, the place where Brian and I talked the most, the place where Brian and I could be closest, so, the tree house is the eyes and ears of my heart. It is my treasure chest to see and hear.

It was a space for me and Brian that my father built, who was afraid of the basement due to the memory of kidnapping. Now that Brian was with Sua and baby Ian, Brian didn't need to climb the tree house nor have time to visit. While Diego was mowing the lawn for the last time, I climbed up to the tree house and was looking back at my past with Brian, who was now a father.

It seemed that Diego finished mowing the lawn as the noise

disappeared. But when I got down from the tree house and looked around, he was nowhere to be seen. He was probably putting the machine into the warehouse. Diego knew the equipment warehouse better than my family, so he had a chainsaw, long pruning shears, and a lawn mower on display whenever needed.
Thanks to Diego, no one in my family paid any attention to the household chores that men usually perform, but now that he was leaving, I felt really sad.

My father would be saddened more than anyone else. My father believed in him to the extent that he told Brian that it is a great blessing to meet a faithful person in life.
What I would miss about Diego, though I haven't talked to him often, is perhaps that he and I shared a similar skin tone and appearance, a look that, no matter how assimilated, we'll never be like Brian. And most of all, it must have been because he and I were in the same situation living away from home.

After dinner, my parents were watching TV in the living room, and Brian was reading a book with baby Ian on his lap. As Sua and I were about to enjoy the tea we prepared, the doorbell rang. Some had their eyes on the TV, some had their eyes on a book, but they looked at each other, 'Who is it at this hour?' I was thinking it would be Diego.
"Welcome, Diego."
I opened the door. Diego was standing there holding a bunch of Chrysanthemum.
"Excuse me for coming at such a late hour."
After a moment's hesitation, Diego entered the room and handed a bunch of flowers in his hand to me. "Thank you,"I accepted.
"Would you like a cup of tea for Diego?"
Before my father and mother could speak at the same time, I had already prepared a teacup.

While preparing the tea, I thought that Diego might say goodbye. What was his main job that required him to return to the vineyards for several years?
I was sad again thinking that I wouldn't be able to see Diego next year. It was because those who came were welcome, but those who go out left a mark on the hearts of those who remained. Diego would leave

many marks in our hearts as he had shown.
"Now that the year has ended well, the day is coming when you'll return to your hometown?"
My mother started the usual, friendly conversation, and my father said, "Good job, Diego."
"Thank you so much, it has been a good experience over the years."
"No, you're talking like you're never coming back?" said my mother
"Actually, I'm going to quit my farm work this year."
"You quit, why?"
My father straightened his back.
"Now when I go back, I want to do what I have to do. It was a good experience for me."
Diego said politely, and Brian, who couldn't stand it, said, 'What the hell is that job?'
Diego looked at Brian and smiled once.
"Actually, I am writing. I envision a scene where many Mexicans come to Canada to work. I had to know farm work for my novel. It took a little longer as I was working."
"Are you a writer?"
"Yes."
Diego smiled.
"Oh my God, we didn't know, you were a writer!"
Mother had an apologetic expression on her face that she made a writer do something too harsh.
"I'm not a famous writer. I wanted to know the relationship between farm owners and workers, how different cultures meet and help each other, and how workers from far away countries are treated in this land, in what environment, and in what kind of work they do. Based on my experiences, I needed time to refine the finished draft more intensively, so I will stop working on the farm."
Diego said softly. Diego was a very good talker.
"You surprise people."
Not only my father, but everyone in the family looked at him with admiration.
"I am at an age where I still need experience, so I have learned a lot while working with the elderly."
"You have surprised me many times, Diego."
Brian said.

"Oh, I was rude last time, Brian. And I also wanted to say thank you to Anna."
When Diego said he was rude, my father and mother looked at Brian with curious expressions, but Brian and Diego only laughed.
"I sincerely thank you two for trusting me with all the household chores. I want to thank you again in my novel for what you have given me."
"Wait, haven't we ever made you sad?"
Everyone laughed when my father joked.
"Yeah, what kind of writing do you do, Diego?"
My mother asked the specific genre of the work.
"I am writing a novel. There is love and parting in the world of working on a farm. There are hardships in life, but there is hope and betrayal waiting for people who have to work half a year in another country, leaving their families in their hometown. I made money while working on this project, so now I want to focus on writing."
"Awesome, Diego! You seem to be enjoying life doing whatever you want to do."
My mother exclaimed.
"But don't think it's the last time and you're welcome to come again anytime. We will miss you."
My father also had a very sad look on his eyes.
"Yes, sir, someday I will bring you my finished book. I also mow the lawn when it is mowing season."
"I'll leave the lawn unmowed until Diego arrives!"
We laughed again at my mother's joke.
Diego was still in front of me, but I kept missing him.

10. Meeting Him

As winter deepened, the family often gathered around the fireplace. No matter how much snow covered the road or how cold and harsh the wind blew across the lake, it was warm and bright when the family gathered in one place.
Mother always kept her hands busy with knitting and father found new pleasure. Father sometimes held Ian and looked out the window at the snow-covered vineyards that stretched endlessly. And with baby Ian in his arms, the father said,
'Ian, look at that vineyard. It's yours.'
It was like my father's own ritual to instill a sense of ownership in his grandson's young heart by showing the vineyards lined up in an endless, orderly line.
'Father held my hand when I was little and he used to say, 'look, Brian, it's yours. When I was growing up, I knew I had to become the owner of a vineyard.'
Brian once told me.

Father and mother met on a boat carrying immigrants from England to Canada. At that time my father was sixteen and my mother was fifteen. A mint candy that my father gave to Joanne, who was sick on the boat, became a bond and the two got married. Later, father and mother settled in this town starting with a small farm, but now it had expanded to a large farm and winery where workers from Mexico or Jamaica came to work. All of this would have been for Brian.
One day, Brian said to Father, 'I don't want to make people drunk with wine, Dad.' Those were words that could have crushed his father's old, grand dreams.
'Brian, everything requires moderation. No matter how good the

food, if you eat too much, you will get an upset stomach. The reason I make wine is to make people enjoy it, not to get drunk. When you are happy, when you are in trouble, when you need comfort, a glass of wine is more than wine. But moderation is up to each individual.'
That was my father's philosophy on alcohol. Brian was tempted a lot by alcohol, but he never went too far. As Father said, he was just having fun.
Now Father was telling baby Ian what he had said to Brian. Whether Ian understood his grandfather or not, my father opened the morning by repeating to his grandson what he had told Brian. Now that it started, Ian would naturally have a sense of ownership of the farm by listening to his grandfather. And he would feel responsible.

Brian had been to China for the wine business and even went to Korea, where he had been for three years. When Brian went to Korea, Sua wanted to go too with her baby, Ian, but she gave up saying that it would not be easy for her to travel long distances because Ian was still young.

As winter deepened, my mother, who did not go out often, knitted a fur hat and gloves that the baby could wear when he grew up, and Sua, who was breast-feeding, continued to eat.

"Oh my, I've gained weight again, Anna!"
Even though she was surprised by the weight she gained whenever she stood on the scale, Sua was constantly eating something.

"I'm glad you ate well, Sua. You had to eat for two. What if you gain some weight? It's okay, you can exercise when it's time for Ian to stop breastfeeding. When that time comes, the three of us should go swimming.'
My mother served cooked fruit, and Sua said, 'No way..' but she continued to eat.
I got permission from Sua and carried baby Ian.
When I said that I wanted to carry Ian, saying, "In the past, mothers in Peru also raised babies by carrying them", Sua put Ian on my back and tied a blanket around my waist.

As winter deepened, I sometimes thought of Diego, whom I might never see again. Above all, I was curious about his novel, the story of the experience he had here. Did he say that there was love and hope and betrayal in the world of farm workers from other countries? The rumors that Brian and I made seemed to be part of the story. If so, I wondered how the rumor was described in a fictional story in Diego's imagination. As a reader, I waited for his novel, which had not yet been published.

And as winter deepened, my mother and I made food that the family enjoyed. I occasionally played the zamponya. I couldn't go to the hibernating tree house, so when I played the zamponya from my room looking at Lake Ontario through the window, Sua came and listened.

'I'm in tears, Anna.'

Sua really shed tears.

'I think I can see why Brian said he wanted to cry when he heard Anna play the zamponya.'

Saying that, Sua pulled up tears from her deep, well-like eyes.

On the way home from the winery, the maple trees lined up on both sides had already put on and took off snow coats over and over again. The trees swayed as if they were about to fall in the wind of Lake Ontario. But, the bare branches of the short vines were connected with wires and were wintering together. The vine never fell, no matter how harsh the winter wind that was running over the lake scratched them. That day too, I was playing the zamponya in my room, songs my brother Mario enjoyed. When I started playing <The Lonely Shepherd> after finishing <El Condor Pasa>, Sua knocked and said, 'Answer the phone, Anna'.

I stopped playing and went downstairs. My mother waved the receiver at me.

"Take the call. It's Michael."

My mother said it was Michael, but as I suddenly heard the name, I was a little confused who Michael was. Because no one by the name of Michael would call me.

"It's Michael."

Mother handed the receiver to me and spoke in a low voice. She had a very strange expression on her face, like a mixture of tension and curiosity.

'That Michael, the Michael of childhood?'

I was asking my mother with my eyes and at the same time my heart was pounding, so I took a deep breath and told the person on the phone, 'It's Anna Hills.'

"Anna!"

A man named Michael called out my name "Anna" as if he had a very friendly relationship with me. Then he said nothing. It must have been a phone call because he had something to say, but when I answered it, he didn't say anything.

“Michael Evans?”

After taking a deep breath, I calmly called out his name.

“Yes, this is Michael. How are you, Anna Hills?”

That voice was definitely not the voice of Michael, a young Michael, the mischievous Michael who was making fun of me.

"I was worried you wouldn’t call, but thank you for getting back to me.”

Little by little, Michael began to speak longer and longer.

“What are you calling for?”

I spoke in a very formal language.

After hesitating for a while, Michael said, ‘I want to meet you.’

It was then that I remembered Mrs. Gilmore's chatter, Brian's objection, and my grumpy promise to meet Michael. That was last summer.

“Actually... it’s very late, but I wanted to apologize, Anna.”

'Apologize?'

I stood still at the word 'apologize', holding the receiver. Uncomfortable memories that I did not want to recall seemed to arise. Memories that quarreled in my head were things I didn't want to take out. I was afraid that I would run into Michael while walking along the street because we lived in the same neighborhood, but fortunately, it never happened by chance. Last summer, after Mrs. Gilmore had offered to connect Michael with me, I had agreed to come and meet him, but that was not really feasible. It wasn't my sincerity, and above all, because Michael was a bad memory for me, and I wanted to forget even his name. But when he said that he wanted to meet me, that he would apologize, my pounding heart fluttered even more. To calm down, I grabbed the receiver. The palm of the hand that hung the receiver was wet with sweat.

"Yeah? Okay, I deserve that apology, Michael. And I also have something to say.”

So, after making an appointment with Michael, I hung up.

I soon began to regret it. I wondered what I was thinking when I said that I should get an apology from Michael, that I also had something to

say to Michael, I felt as if I was gibberish.
Besides, what do I mean I have something to say? I couldn't understand what I was thinking. What the hell was I trying to say to Michael and that I had something to say to him in the first place. Perhaps it was because I was too nervous.

"Why did Michael call you, Anna?"

My mother Immediately asked with a hardened face. It was because he was not a person who gave my mother a pleasant memory.

"He wants to apologize."

I said with a bit of a calm mind.

"Apologize? Michael? It's not nice to see Michael approaching my daughter again."

I understood the feelings of a mother, who was vigilant from the start. She was a mother who had already been embarrassed in front of her son because of Michael. So Michael was a person who didn't leave pleasant memories for all of us in the family. I started to regret even more after making an appointment to meet Michael to get an apology from him.

"It's only this time. We will never see each other again, Mother."

I promised myself anyway, so I will meet once, but I confidently said that I will never meet him again. Just because Michael, whom I didn't like, apologized, I would never see him again or meet someone who no one in my family welcomed.

On the appointed date and time, I went to a hotel in the neighborhood to meet Michael. This was a hotel where I once went swimming with my mother.

'Well, if Michael is rude again like before, you should stand up and come. Then I'll deal with it.'

As if sending her daughter to the enemy camp, mother asked again and again, and I was pretending to be calm on the outside, but on the inside I was quite nervous.

At this age, I won't be swayed by Michael again, but my attitude in accepting the promise that I'll meet him to meet me for the first time caught my heart again and again. I wondered how much more Michael would have changed since he became an adult. But since I came all the way here, I thought I should accept his apology and come out as soon as I'm done talking with him. I went into the hotel.

There were many empty tables in the hotel lounge where a fireplace

was burning.
Without looking, I sat down at a table with the fireplace behind me. When the waiter came up to me and asked if I would like to order a drink, I thought about waiting for Michael, but I ordered coffee. It was because I didn't want to be so polite.

Michael, how could I forget him? When I was seven years old, I came to this land with my new parents, and when my parents and Brian made me go to school, it was Michael who had been close to me ever since. Michael was taller than Brian and the two were friends. But they got along badly because Michael bullied me.

'Anna, why are you different?'

'Go to your house, Anna!'

'Why can't you speak, you are dumb!'

As I understand only Quechua, I can only guess what Michael meant by the teasing sound he made around me, and I couldn't argue with him or tell him not to do it to me. Whenever Michael did that, I sat down and sat still, covering my face.

'Anna is an idiot!'

He pulled my braided hair, and then from nowhere, Brian appeared, wheezing and clenching his fists in front of Michael.

'Don't do that to Anna!'

When Brian couldn't force Michael, who was taller than himself, and when Brian only confronted Michael with his words, Michael made fun of Brian, 'What are you, Brian? Why are you different from Anna?' Even Brian, who was so patient, once attacked Michael with force. He suddenly appeared and swiped Michael down.
The two had to be called to the teacher's office but Michael's teasing still continued. So, even if Brian heard only the name of Michael, Brian was terrified, and he was against it, fearing that he might get involved with me.

It was Michael who had asked me to meet him. I was here and he'd be sitting somewhere if he came first, but I didn't look. It would be nice if Michael recognized me and came over here, but I didn't want to look around the room to find him.
I took a sip after adding milk and sugar to the coffee the waiter had brought. The tension seemed to have eased a bit. It didn't seem like Michael had arrived yet and no one who sat around recognized me until the waiter brought my coffee.

After swimming, I sometimes visited this lounge with my mother.
'Anna, coffee tastes better when I pay for it.'
Every time we visited this place, my mother and I were of one mind, like conspirators. When we became one from something small, my mom was as happy as a little girl.
"Are you Anna Hills?"
I forgot about Michael for a moment and while I was sipping sweet coffee like I did when I was here with my mother, a man called my name. He was tall, with short sideburns covering his cheeks. It was then that I woke up and remembered that I was waiting for someone.
"Michael?"
I called his name. He nodded and looked down at me with a look that seemed to be very humble and very happy.
"Can I sit down?"
He was getting my permission and I was thinking for a second that this wasn't Michael.
"Of course."
At the same time as I said, Michael pulled the chair back a little and sat across from me. My heart was pounding and it felt like it was trembling, but I took a deep breath.
"Actually, I saw you when you came in and I sat down for a while to relax."
Michael's voice was soft and kind. Him asking was a more honest expression than I expected, so I looked at Michael.
Michael has changed so much that I would not have recognized him if we had passed by on the street. My worries that I might meet him by chance were nothing but futile.
"I wanted to apologize, Anna. Sorry. It was a shame."
Michael's temper was a bit impatient, so before he even ordered coffee, he adjusted his posture and said 'I'm sorry'. I had a feeling that it was the sincere attitude of a person who had been feeling sorry for a long time.
'Sorry'
When I heard it, 'I'm sorry' was the second sorry I heard from a man. Brian's words at the snowy dawn that day were 'I'm sorry'. Brian and Michael's 'sorry' had different meanings, but as I listened, I was thinking, 'Sorry' is a very convenient word. 'I'm sorry' was one word that made it seem like it never happened even if it hurt the other

person's heart.

The power of those short words was so strong that I had to relax my mind when Brian, who I knew as the only person, suddenly put Sua in front of my eyes one day and said 'I'm sorry'. And even though the uncomfortable memories that have followed me since I was a child were still vivid in my mind, I had to forgive Michael with a single word of 'I'm sorry'.

'You should get an apology from Michael. Don't lose your mind when he apologizes, Anna.'

These were the words of my mother, who was more vigilant than I was at Michael's call. My mother was worried about what else Michael might say to me.

But did my heart become soft? The moment I heard Michael say 'I'm sorry', it seemed that the old feelings in my heart had melted away. It was probably because it all happened in the past.

"It's very late, but will you forgive me, Anna?"

Michael's blue eyes were like the color of Lake Ontario when the sky descended on a clear day.

'Are you really asking for forgiveness in front of me? Is this really Michael?'

I asked myself.

The man in front of me was really Michael, that bully Michael.

'What changed Michael like this?'

I was asking myself again, because I couldn't believe it.

At this point, I had to say something. I made it clear that I had something to say and indeed it was my turn to say something.

"We were all young. I just wanted to say this Michael."

Because he was young, he could do it, because he was immature, so he could be forgiven.

I thought, in the eyes of Michael when he was young, my appearance could be the reason for curiosity and a reason for teasing. My eyes were different from those of Michael's blue eyes and the skin color and appearance were definitely different.

I decided to see Michael's point of view when he was young and to understand Michael's immature words and actions. I had forgotten my mother's words not to open my heart.

"Oh, thank you Anna. Anna, you have become a wonderful lady"

Michael's voice, already relieved of tension, was pleasant.
'Michael, you have changed a lot too,'I was saying to myself.
I let go of my old feelings so quickly that it overshadowed the fact that for so many years I had suppressed a deep resentment in my heart. Even though my mother had warned me not to, I had loosened the boundaries of my heart sooner than I had planned.

I began to think, what really made the bullying boy change into a young man who could admit his mistake and apologize. It was time. It must have been time to make him regret his unstoppable behavior even if he told himself not to do it and to let him know that he was sorry to himself. The time that passed in front of Michael and I, that long period of time, gave Michael the courage to say 'I'm sorry' and gave him space to 'understand'.

"How could we have never met while living in the same neighborhood?"
As if curious, Michael said as he drank coffee.
It was fortunate for me that I had never met him. If I had bumped into Michael all of a sudden on the street or at a restaurant, there would not have been such an opportunity for an apology and it may not have been possible for me to think of the memories back in time, because I would have hated Michael all the time.

"Yeah."
I slightly agreed with Michael's words. After passing the moment of 'Sorry and Forgiveness', a lot of old stories went back and forth between us. Michael and I had common stories of studying in the same neighborhood and at the same school.
As Michael spoke, he asked me, 'What do you think?' several times. It seemed to be a habit of Michael's words, but it had the same meaning as Michael's wish, 'I hope you think the same as me...', so whenever that happened, I just laughed.

"Anna, I want to see you again, what do you think?"
When Michael said it again as we were about to leave, I was momentarily conflicted because I promised my mother that once I got an apology, I would never see Michael again. That's how I felt at the time, that I would never see Michael again, how could I?
But the reason my heart was conflicted was that I did not want to reject Michael's request at this very moment. But now, I wanted to see him again. I was smiling at Michael, rationalizing that it would not be

too late to say ‘no!’ if I don't want to meet him again.
Perhaps because it wasn't the word 'No,' Michael's expression brightened like a child. So, when Michael asked again, ‘Are we going to meet again?’ I easily answered, 'Yeah,'
On the way home, thinking about it, I think I laughed a lot more than I thought. To meet Michael and laugh, was it magic created by time? It seemed impossible to say 'no'.

“Are you okay, Anna?”
My mother was waiting for me at the door. My mother's eyes were mingled with curiosity and concern. My mother was worried that her daughter would get hurt again, but she must have been a little curious as it was a meeting between a man and a woman who are now adults.
“How was your first date, Anna?”
Sua said it was Anna's first date, and begged me to tell her today's story.
“Okay, talk to us, Anna. We have been waiting for you to come.”
“Michael was like a different person,”
I said with a smile. He really was. We waited at different tables in the hotel lounge, but I didn't recognize Michael and he said he already recognized me and sat down a bit to deal with the tension. He said 'sorry' first.
I told my mother all of that.
“So, you mean he wasn’t the old Michael?”
“That was when Michael was immature...”
When my mother looked into my eyes and insisted on me, my sudden reply was an excuse for Michael. It was strange that I was making excuses for Michael with a smile on my face. The way I smiled when I was talking about Michael was something I couldn't even imagine myself. My mother was staring into my eyes. My mother had a look that found a different feeling in my expression.
“It’s fortunate that Michael has grown into a good young man. Mrs. Evans suffered a lot with Michael, but now it's all gone."
My mother was relieved.
“I want to see him again, Mother.”
“Anna!”
Calling me, mother couldn't speak. Her expression looked like a rebuke to me, 'What happened after you said you'd never see Michael again?' Perhaps my mother was astonished by her daughter's change of heart.

Sua had a wide smile. She looked as if she knew the change in my heart. Despite Brian's steadfast objection, I suddenly offered to meet Michael as if I was throwing myself away, but after that I had forgotten about it.

'Last summer, after hearing Mrs. Gilmore's words, I wanted to call you, but I didn't have the courage. There were too many things I did wrong to Anna.'

That's what Michael said. So Michael had already heard the stories of the women's meeting that day through Mrs. Gilmore.

"My daughter couldn't say 'no'. Yes, I think I can understand that feeling. But let's not rush."

It seemed that my mother was slowly calming my heightened emotions that I had never had before.

Even though Michael and I met frequently, I didn't get a suitable opportunity to say 'No!'.

My heart started to take an interest in Michael. As I met Michael, I began to feel more and more curious as if I had never known Michael from the beginning.

In fact, my curiosity about Michael was a radical change. It was then that I began to think that Brian must have been like this when he met Sua.

11. First Kiss

When Michael's work was over, it was time for us to meet. After driving together, we ate and went to the movies on the weekends. Since winter was still lingering, those were all we could do together. Michael was still careful around me and I still thought that I needed to know more about him and if I didn't like him, I had to say 'No' any time. We were hesitant and careful because we couldn't get closer to each other due to the past.

Michael asked me to ride a bike along the parkway when winter was over, then he said he would like to ride a boat with me as soon as possible. It was still winter, but he waited for summer. Michael seemed to think our meeting would last until summer.

Brian was the only man I knew until I met Michael. Growing up with Brian, the world of men I experienced was the only thing I knew. But the stories Michael told me were from a world I didn't know. It was a story of a home and family in a different environment, a story of growing up different from Brian, a story of different hobbies and work, and even stories of alcoholism and treatment.

Michael told stories that were very unfamiliar to me that I had the illusion that he had many stories he wanted to tell, but no one had ever listened to him. As I was listening to Michael's story, I fell in love with Michael's story just as Sua was absorbed in Brian's story.

Still, rather than the man named Michael, it was his stories that captivated me. And I waited for the next story, which meant that I was starting to open up more and more towards Michael.

Maybe Michael felt the same way as I, so when we parted, he always said, 'I don't know how time flies when I'm with you Anna.' Then he said, 'I want to meet you tomorrow too, but what do you think?' After confirming my thoughts and receiving my answer, he went home.

Both of us were already adults, but the way Michael got his next date was like a child. If we had a good relationship with each other, I thought he wouldn't use that expression when we met and parted. Through his language habits, I thought that Michael might be a more naive person than I thought.
No matter how much I had accumulated negative feelings for Michael, if he looked at me straight and asked me these questions every day. It seemed like I would never be able to answer 'No!'. Far from saying 'No!' The more I met him, the more curious I got as I got to know him. It meant that I wanted to meet him as much as Michael did.

We met often in the old hotel lounge where we first met. With the fireplace close by, we ate and drank tea and stayed for hours.
'I liked Uncle Ted a lot and followed him around a lot.'
That day Michael talked about his uncle Ted. His father's younger brother, Ted, lived alone and had taken Michael like his son ever since Michael was a child.
'I wanted to do everything Uncle Ted did. He was good at fishing, so I wanted to be good at fishing and he was good at skiing, so I waited for winter. Uncle Ted also enjoyed hunting too.'
'Michael, did you hunt too? Did you kill animals with a gun?'
I was imagining Michael aiming his gun at the head of a deer that was carelessly picking berries. It was truly a terrible imagination.
'No, no, Anna, I hate hunting!'
Michael smirked like a child and waved his hands, saying no.
'I've never been on a hunt. Actually, I was a little scared. When Uncle Ted went fishing, he always took me with him, but the condition was that he never let me pierce the earthworm with a fishing rod. I didn't like earthworms, but I really hated tying live things to fishing hooks. Then Uncle Ted said, 'Michael, now you can easily buy fishing worms in the store, but when I was a kid, I went fishing after catching worms in the middle of the night on the lawn.'
So, what he meant was that a person who can't even touch an earthworm can't even shoot an animal, so I believed Michael's words.
Michael's father was also reluctant to kill animals with a gun, so he was dissatisfied with Uncle Ted's hunting habit, but Michael's uncle said that it was permitted by the government under a license and he went hunting to the north during hunting season.
'No one in the family touched a gun. Uncle kept it in a box with a

lock in his house, but he never showed me the gun. Uncle Ted knew I wanted to imitate anything he did.'
'If it were me, I don't think I would ever follow.'
Aiming a gun at a deer was terrifying, no matter how I thought about it.
'Do you think so too? I really liked everything Uncle Ted did, but hunting was a hobby of his I never wanted to imitate. If I ever wanted to follow him, it was probably because I wanted to become an ant.'
'Ant? Ah!'
Realizing what he meant, I let out a sound of admiration without realizing it. Because Michael was talking about a fairy tale. A dove dropped a leaf to save an ant that was floating in the water, but one day the pigeon was in danger of being shot by a hunter.
The ant went into the hunter's pants and bit the hunter. The hunter's gun missed. It was Aesop's fable about the ant rescuing the dove and returning the favor.
As I listened to Michael's version of the fable, I was thinking, Michael had read a lot and he was a witty and persuasive person who adapted the stories he read to.
And I thought, "If that time comes, I should say 'No!' to Michael, but I might not be able to say 'No!' to him. It was because of his warm heart that I didn't know existed until now.
One word, 'Ant', which he said casually, made me look at Michael more carefully and with a happy heart. It was as if the root of a long and deeply entrenched dislike in me was shaken by that one little word.

When we parked the car by the river while driving through the parkway, the car was our own space. The car was a music room, a coffee shop with hot coffee. And though we were not in that relationship yet, how did we know whether this would be the space for our first kiss.
In Lake Ontario and Niagara River, boats of various shapes and sizes started to show up from late spring to early fall, but the air was still cold, so people put their boats in their backyards and waited for the season to come. Instead of boats in the river, goose and other flocks of birds with their hips raised, plunged into the cold water to catch fish.
"I'm going to ride a boat in the summer."
Michael said, looking out over the river, where flocks of birds were swaying with the wind-swept waves.

"There are several types of boats. There is a Sea Doo called an underwater motorcycle, an outboard that mounts the motor on the outside of the back of the boat, an inboard that mounts the motor on the inside of the front of the boat and a flat square deck. There's also something called a Pontoon Boat with an awning. The speed boat I enjoy is also called a cigar boat and the motor is usually mounted on the inside. When the weather gets warmer, come ride with me, Anna. You will love it too."
Apparently, Michael was convinced that we could be together in the summer.

"I've been drinking since my teenage years."
Michael suddenly talked about alcohol.
Michael's remarks, I thought, must have been something that Michael's mother, Mrs. Evans, had just stopped confessing at the ladies' meeting, which had spread through the neighborhood and finally reached my ears.
Since this was Michael's personal life, I looked at him a little nervously.
"At first I drank secretly without my parents knowing, but later I drank at the winery or anywhere at home. After drinking every day, I suddenly thought, "Why am I always drinking?" I have good parents and my sincere older brother is going well on his way. Was it dissatisfaction with an environment that could not be satisfied? In the end it was because of myself."
'From a young age, I was overly mean-spirited, and my grumpiness got tougher. It was a vicious cycle of being dissatisfied with myself. As a way to avoid myself, I drank a little at first, then gradually fell in love with it, and then I drank too much, and there were too many drinks around me.
My will was too weak to ignore temptation. Still, I often asked myself, 'What the hell am I dissatisfied with?' The cause was always within me. I knew the answer, but I lacked patience. In the end, weakness was the problem."
Michael started pouring out even the hard parts, as if 'Now, Anna, I believe in you and want to reveal everything to you.'

"Riding a boat was to kind of show that I wasn't weak. Not to enjoy speed, but to cover my weaknesses. As I cut through the water and the air with speed, I got a feeling of wanting to blow away all of my

weakness. In the summer, I almost lived in the water and that was an opportunity to avoid drinking even for a while."
Michael had made many attempts on his own to break free from his weakness.

"It was very fortunate that I got to know myself a bit. To cover my weakness, I made others suffer. When I wasn't satisfied with that, I drank and hid behind alcohol. Now that I think about it, it was such a stupid and childish thing to do, but at the time I didn't know any other way. There were things like my parents' interest and good teaching, but I didn't pay any attention to them. I acted against my family who were trying to guide me on the right path and I made my family cry and I blamed myself. I would have shattered every single thing, like the happiness and fantasy of parents raising children.
I always thought, ``Why do I live this way", I don't want to live this way, but then I thought, "What should I do?" I thought of ways to avoid drinking and it drove me to boat, bike, and run.

"When I think about it, I think I made up my mind very harshly. I've never beat myself up by trying something, so knowing me a little bit would have helped me overcome myself. I don't want to live with myself like that anymore."

Michael was slowly telling me the story of his past, the time he wanted to hide. It was the story of Michael, who had a hard life, being swayed by himself more than he had tormented me. It was a story of a painful time for a weak young man.

Nevertheless, the reason that the story drew my heart was because it was the story of how he struggled to overcome the pain and finally overcame it. It was because the story was positive and hopeful, overcoming one's own shortcomings by finding the cause of pain in oneself rather than in others or in the environment.

"Michael, you are a very strong person."
I sincerely thought so. When Michael revealed his own weakness that was buried deep inside, I changed my childhood prejudices about him into the image of a strong Michael who knew and overcame his own weaknesses.

If Michael had tried to show me what he had, how much he enjoyed himself, and how confident he was, I would have been disappointed. Far from discovering Michael's charm. Because I would never have seen the change of character that time had made in him.

"Michael, you are a great man, because you have beaten yourself."
"I've been tormenting you a lot, but you give me courage instead of resentment, Anna."
"I told you, it was all because we were young."
Michael quietly looked into my eyes.
"Since I met you, there are times when I think about wanting to be a good person. Am I a little childish?"
Michael chuckled. He was really like a little kid, a very naive boy.
"Yeah, you look like a very naive boy, so I want to hug him."
It was my sincerity. How easy was it to reveal his dark past, especially in front of a woman? It is not possible without childish innocence and sincere courage. So, in my eyes, Michael was a nice guy.
"Now, can you hug me?"
Michael begged like a child. He was like a cute boy.
"Yes, I will give you a hug."
I hugged Michael without hesitation. And I put my lips on his forehead. To me, Michael was a wonderful boy who did a great job.
Michael, who quietly held me in his chest, embraced me as if it was his turn this time. He stood still, embraced, and gently pressed his lips to my cheek. Michael's lips, which had hesitated for a moment on my cheek, found mine as if he didn't want to be a boy anymore.
Michael's lips, which met mine, hesitated for a moment and then began to move violently. From a boy's lips to the lips of a man, he began to lust after mine. My lips happily met Michael's. This was because we had already gone through all those processes and were now meeting as man and woman.
It was in his car on the Niagara River that we became one with our lips.

12. Proposal

That's how I spent the winter, meeting Michael. Were winters in Canada this short? Winter always seemed like spring that came and went in a hurry. Maybe I was unaware of the boundaries of the seasons because I met Michael every day and spent time as brightly as the spring sunshine. It wasn't that winter was particularly short, but it seemed like it because my mind was elsewhere.

I spent winter like spring and when the workers returned from Jamaica and Mexico to work on the farm, around the time when the lovely spring flowers were prying their faces through the still cold ground, Michael proposed. He opened the ring box to me in the car, not at the restaurant he was running, but on the parkway.

"Anna Hills, I just wanted to tell you here at this place where you first hugged me and we kissed for the first time. I want to live with you for a long time."

It was definitely a proposal. What did Michael mean when he said 'I want to live with you for a long time' if not 'I want to marry you'?

Only a season had passed since the two of us first met, explored, knew, and convinced each other.

My innate nature and my influences from my environment combined to create me, Anna Hills. But what did Michael, who met me in one season, one of the shortest of those long hours, believe in and want to live with me for a long time?

And I still had nightmarish memories of my childhood that I never wanted to look back on. But how can I trust him and accept his offer? Do we know each other enough to be sure of each other?

Even if we knew each other, marriage might be a gamble for both of us. If I looked only at the negative aspects, it would have been a gamble

that could carry a huge risk. Did I really want to gamble my life?
When Michael said he wanted to live with me, in the car where we held and kissed for the first time, many questions arose in my mind, but I looked at Michael without saying a word for a moment. As if Michael's blue eyes were a movie screen, the memories of the film in my head were projected through Michael's eyes and passed quickly.

My mother, who died while giving birth to my younger brother, passed by first, and my brother, Mario, who was playing the zamponya, and my father, who caught the turcha at Lake Titicaca and came home with the sunset behind his back, passed by.
Then, the child who called me “Anna!” who was “Mamani” in her childhood, and Brian, who I thought would be the only man in my life, stayed on the screen of Michael’s eyes for a while.

A man out of nowhere was offering a ring to me, who only dreamed of having my first kiss, proposal, and marriage with him.

The child, who tormented me in my childhood, the child I was afraid of running into on the way, the child who deeply wounded me when I was young so that my heart could not be friendly, and as Brian said, a young man who revealed the hardship he had to endure at a young age, and Michael, who could not rule out the possibility that he might fall into the swamp again at any time, wanted to live with me for a long time at this moment.

Was he tormenting me with sweet words with a ring in front of my eyes, just like when we were kids? Did this make any sense? Was this even possible?
If it was for an absolutely absurd reason, if it was only for the words and deeds that tortured me until the end, it seemed that it would be okay for me to slap him on the back or even slash him in the cheek. Maybe I can do that for once? It was clear that the one word ‘sorry’ and ‘you were young’ was said too easily. So he must’ve been talking nonsense again.

But the problem was, while it definitely didn’t make sense, I couldn't say, 'Michael, why are you talking nonsense like that?' Instead of saying something, tears welled up first. Tears, no matter how much I cried, I couldn't help but wonder how ridiculous this was at this point in time.

But why did the tears come first? Why did my eyes respond before my lips? I was certainly not sad and I couldn't have been more sad, but the tears that had started to flow from my eyes started to flow out of control.

"Are you okay, Anna?"Michael asked, not knowing what to do. It felt like something was springing up inside. But I couldn't say anything.

'Anna, why are you crying?'

I couldn't control myself either. What was wrong with me? Unable to handle this uncontrollable rumbling in my heart, I finally started crying while covering my face with both hands. I wept and said,

"Yes, I will live with you. Michael, I want to live with you for a long time!"

And then I held out my hand. No matter how much I thought about it, it seemed that the direction of my heart was the answer rather than calculating the risks.

Michael, bewildered by my tears, smiled and put the ring on my finger. Michael was already in tears.

"You're a crybaby, Anna."

Michael said as he hugged me and kissed my wet cheek. On my finger was a ring like my teardrops. It was a drop of joy.

"That Michael..."

When I told my family about Michael's proposal, my mother's expression looked very complicated and subtle. It seemed to mean "why is it Michael?", or that our daughter had been proposed to by Michael, and it also seemed to contain feelings of parents unsure of sending their daughter to Michael. Brian kept his mouth shut.

"How can I let my daughter go!"

My mother shed tears first. Those tears must have been tears of joy, tears of disappointment, and tears of many meanings.

"I am glad that Michael has grown into a good young man. It's a good thing that our families know each other well.'

It seemed that my parents only wanted to think positively.

"I thought it was going to be like this, Anna."

Sua smiled broadly. She seemed to like my wedding news more than I.

"Anna looked happy from the first day."

Sua had the look of the woman who was in love. Although my parents and Sua were rather excited and had laughter on their faces, Brian only said one word, 'Congratulations, Anna.' and he was silent the whole time.

From the day after accepting Michael's proposal, we were the happiest couple in the world.
I became more and more talkative. Like the day I met Michael, I was no longer the quiet Anna. My mother said, 'Love changes my daughter like this. It's like looking back at me a long time ago." My mother looked at me curiously.
It was my mother and father who became a couple after a mint candy given by a 16-year-old boy to a fifteen-year-old girl who was suffering from motion sickness on a boat immigrating to Canada with her family. My mother, who still lived life like a love affair, seemed to think of the time when Father proposed to her with a candy.
“Anna, your mother is always happy because you are our daughter. Now is the time to share that happiness with Michael. But I hope you never forget that we are behind you.”
My Peruvian mother passed away early and my childhood memories of living with my brother and father were like old photos. As I became the daughter of my step-parents in Canada and Brian's older sister, my body and mind grew up during the time I lived with them. So now it was clear that I was my mother's daughter.
Brian, however, spoke less. Brian couldn't say anything about things that had already been confirmed. I understood that he was talking less as he had to sort out his inner grievances on his own. I was the one who knew Brian best. If Michael and I were happy, Brian would change his mind. I decided to think of Brian as my younger brother's interest in his older sister. That was how it had to be.

13. Their Story

Michael and I made a promise to get married in early June, when the cherries were turning red, but not too hot in the summer. When he said 'I'm sorry,' I also said, 'We were young back then,' and we met to apologize and forgive each other. That was our beginning. We approached each other with hesitation and as our meeting led to the next meeting, we finally made a marriage promise.

June in Ontario was both a ripe spring and an unripe summer. It was the season to enjoy the fresh green and flowers, where living things could enjoy the sunlight, cool wind, and fresh air to their heart's content. The cherries were turning red and by the end of June the farm would put out cherry-picking signs. People enjoyed the cherry season by climbing up the ladder and picking cherries, peach, apricot, and plum, while grapes and apples ripened slowly.

'We are busy with farm work, but the marriage of our children has made us even busier.'

My mother and Michael's mother, Mrs. Evans, exchanged words of encouragement to each other and shared happy thoughts and both fathers were of the same mind.

"The wedding will be held in our yard. We want to do everything Brian couldn't do.'

'The house for the children to live in is already ready, Joanne."

The opinions of the two mothers matched each other like the palms of their hands.

'Okay. I hope it doesn't rain that day.'

'If it rains on the wedding day, they will become rich.'

Then the two wives laughed. The two wives, who only wanted to think good thoughts, put a positive interpretation on everything and

it seemed that their relationship became stronger because they were going to be in-laws.
Before the wedding, there was one thing I wanted to do. It was just meeting Brian. Although we see each other at home every day, I wanted to see him alone this time. I wanted to say thank you for protecting me, for being my younger brother until now. And I wanted to tell him not to worry.

I went to the winery where Brian worked. It was the season when tourists were starting to come in, so Brian was busier than ever. Although commercial liquor stores sold various types of wine produced by our winery, tourists from other countries or other regions also came to the winery to taste and buy wine that touched their taste, so Brian took care of all that as the owner.

"Brian, I'm here."

"What's going on, Anna?"

Brian, talking to an employee, was happy to see me. Brian seemed to be gradually becoming a businessman. Father also taught him management after Brian came from Korea. In my opinion, Brian's personality was more suited to research and experiment in a laboratory rather than a business, but Brian understood the reality that he had to inherit the family business.

"I came to see you."

Brian and I were now able to exchange words that made our hearts tremble as lightly as jokes. It was an inevitable change.

"Wow, my heart is pounding, Anna!"

I walked into the office while Brian was making coffee. It was the place where father worked for a long time and now it was the place where Brian mainly worked.

On Brian's desk, there was a computer, a picture of baby Ian smiling broadly as if he was about to burst out of laughter and a picture of Brian and Sua holding Ian. After marrying Michael, I thought that if I had a baby, Michael would put a picture like that on his desk. Now in Brian's office, thinking of Michael and not Brian, I was feeling a change of heart. Brian and I eventually went our separate ways, so why did we miss, annoy, and hurt so much? I now saw the reason for our irreversible relationship, not from Brian, but from me.

"What is really going on, Anna?"

Brian said in a cheerful voice, holding the coffee.

"I have a lot to say to you."
Brian looked up at me at my words. In fact, Brian must have known everything that was going on in my relationship with Michael. He just kept quiet about it.
For a moment, Brian and I were just holding coffee.
"Are your wedding preparations going well?"
Brian asked about the wedding first. This was Brian's way of trying to ease me, as I was having a hard time speaking up. A bitter longing arose. It was Brian who always thought of me first. He had to suffer because of me, he left for Korea because of me, and he never hesitated to argue in front of his parents because of me. He spoke first for me, because I would be embarrassed to speak.
"Yes."
I answered briefly. It was Brian who guessed my heart even with a single word.
"So? It's going fine. What's up?"
What Brian meant was that everything was going well, so why bother?
"I just wanted to tell you not to worry about me. Until now, because of me, you've done too much..."
I was about to say something, but tears fell.

How can I think of my adopted life without Brian? It started with Brian, I grew up with Brian, I liked and loved Brian, and it was my dream to be with Brian. He was the person who had the greatest influence on my life, the person who was kept in the memory of my precious first love and will still exist as my beloved younger brother.
"It was a precious time that made us who we are. That's how we live our lives, Anna."
Then, putting the cup on the table, he came to me and stroked my cheek, which was already in tears. And he hugged me, saying, 'You have to live well.'
Brian was like my older brother.
"I'm sorry I got married at home."
I sincerely said to Brian who sat down. How much more heartwarming and happier mother and father would have been if their only son, Brian, had married at home. Parents couldn't even attend Brian's wedding in Korea.
"How lucky are our parents to be able to prepare for Anna's wedding to their heart's content? Rather, I want to thank you."

Brian returned to being my younger brother, as he said cheerfully.
"It's all gone, but back then, our parents were very upset. Our parents had high expectations for their trip to Korea as well as attending your wedding."
I was just talking about something that Brian had never mentioned after returning home with Sua. It was about our parents' feelings.

When Brian told our parents that he and Sua had decided to exchange only a wedding ring in Korea and told them not to come, our parents could not understand the reason, and were very upset.
'Anna, have I been so wrong? How did Brian keep his own mother out of my son's wedding?'
At that time, I also thought that Brian's method was not right, and the more Brian did, the more I felt sorry for my parents. It was because Brian's trip to Korea and the marriage there were things that happened because of me. But Brian was so engrossed that he didn't even pretend to caress the sad feelings of his parents, and that was never Brian's way I knew, so I didn't understand either.
'I lost Brian when he was young, but now I think I'll lose him again.'
My mother had not come out of her room for a long time, and because of my mother, my father did not even hide his disappointment with his son.

"I had a problem, Anna."
Brian said, which he had never told his parents as an excuse. But I couldn't ask what it was. It was because there must have been a reason why he had no choice but to do so. And now, that was all over, and my parents kept all of Brian's marriage in their hearts and lived in laughter with baby Ian, Brian and Sua.

"There was a cafe in the building where I taught English and whenever I went there, there was a woman with long hair sitting at the same table."
Brian seemed to be trying to tell the story. I listened to Brian.
"She was a student in my class and after her class she was still sitting there, so I wondered why she wouldn't go home. One day I approached her, asking, 'Shall we have a coffee?', and at the very moment, I was surprised. Her eyes were Anna's."
In Brian's class, she wasn't the student who caught Brian's attention.

“It was the same eyes when I first saw you, Anna, like black grapes. So one day I asked her, why didn't you go home when my class was over? Then she replied, ‘If I leave here now, I don’t think I’ll ever come back.’ Brian said, taking a sip of coffee.

‘Anna’s eyes are like grapes.’
Long ago, when I was called Mamani, Brian, who came to Peru with his family, looked at me and said: ‘Anna’s eyes are like grapes.’
Maybe it was because he was a boy who lived surrounded by vineyards, so when Brian looked into my eyes, he said, 'It's like grapes,' and Brian's mother laughed.
Even my mother didn't know why Brian called me 'Anna', who used to be called 'Mamani'. Mother told me that it was probably because it was easy for Brian call me 'Anna'. From then on, my name changed from Mamani to Anna. Sua's eyes were like black grapes, Brian said.
I also had to take a sip of coffee.
“There's a story behind it,' I guessed. A lady who had a story that she might not come out when she went back home. There was a sense of playfulness within me, that I had to do anything to get her to come to class every day. So I started talking about what I knew best, my country Canada, Lake Ontario, my neighborhood, fishing, orchards, wineries...”
Brian told me again what Sua once told me, 'The next story will be tomorrow', so Brian made Sua wait for the next day. Brian told a story every day, and one day Sua said, 'Your older sister definitely appears in the story.'
“I was caught off guard by Sua. It didn’t matter though, because Sua was just a student in my class. Every day I talked and Sua listened more than my English class and said again, 'You are like Scheherazade'.
At first, I thought about what she meant, but Arabian Nights, which I read in the tree house with you, came to the mind of the woman who saved her life and became a queen.”
Back then, maybe Brian was reading a book on my lap and I was knitting or playing the zamponya. And when Brian fell asleep while reading, I gently pulled the book out of his hand and read it.
‘That was how he grew to love Sua,’
As I listened, I thought that it was Brian's love story.
“But when I was going home after finishing all my work in Korea, Sua made my heart hesitate. I thought my story brightened Sua's heart a

little bit, but when I left, I thought that no one would make Sua want to go out. So I said, I don't want to be Scheherazade anymore, I'll do it my way. So I said I wanted to go to Canada with her and show her everything I said in words."

"Did you propose?"

Proposing to a lover was a wonderful thing that made everyone's heart flutter. It was the same with Michael's proposal to me.

I thought of Michael without hesitation now even in front of Brian.

"It was definitely a proposal, but Sua was asking me. 'How much do you know about me?' Come to think of it, I didn't know anything about Sua because I was always talking. So when I said that I didn't know anything about her, Sua said, 'You are a frivolous person to risk your life without knowing anything about me.' At her resolute refusal, my heart was cut to pieces."

It was Brian who went to Korea with the pain of a love that could not be achieved. And it was surprising to me that Sua had such determination.

So I said, "I couldn't say I knew you if I had heard your whole personal story. What was important to me was not your personal background, but you who had listened to me and talked to me. You've shown me all the important things I need to know. And I said that the things we met and shared at this moment were more important than your past, which I never asked about, and for which I had no reason to know. I said now that my interest was for you to accept my proposal."

Yeah, Brian was such a person, I was thinking. He was a warm, understanding and caring person. He was a nice guy

"But that's when Sua said, 'I've had a failed marriage."

"Sua?"

I shouted in amazement as if someone had splashed ice water on me. Was that why Sua's eyes were so quietly deep?

I said, 'It must have hurt a lot for Sua. I had a love that I couldn't achieve. It hurt a lot. That was the reason I came to Korea. But I didn't think that I couldn't fall in love again because of that. It was the same for Sua. We just had a painful experience that we couldn't make it to the end."

Brian was thinking of returning home with his parents after the wedding, but Sua told Brian the story of what happened at her wedding ceremony.

'On her wedding day, the groom and the bride were standing in front of the officiating man, and the door suddenly opened and a woman with a stroller entered the hall and said, 'Don't do that. He's my baby's dad!'

'The woman's finger was clearly pointing at the man next to me.'

"..!"

I was staring blankly at Brian, unable to say a single word.

'The woman's finger was pointing at the man. And when she said, 'He's my baby's dad,' she was definitely talking to me.'

I was looking at Brian right now, but Sua, who must have been standing in a wedding dress in a frenzy, passed in front of me.

Unspeakable sadness and anger arose within me. The life of a woman who reached the apex of her life, with many people watching, was mercilessly mutilated and crushed to pieces in an instant.

'That's why her eyes were so deep. How could she handle it all?'

Without realizing it, tears welled up in my eyes. Since she had buried her heavy story in such a harsh way, it seemed that she had no choice but to be so deep and quiet.

Without knowing it, I was sorry for the hard work Brian and Sua had in front of them. I felt sorry for the things that made Sua more silent.

"So I couldn't speak. I wanted to put Sua at ease, Anna should be happy with Michael too."

'Oh, Brian, my good brother.'

I looked deeply at Brian. Now I felt like I understood Brian, the circumstances and feelings he could not say anything after making his parents so sad with his wedding. I thought I knew everything, but I didn't know all about Brian.

We looked at each other and smiled.

After filtering out all the hot emotions that were struggling in front of the boundary between siblings, we were younger brother and older sister who were more affectionate than ever before.

14. June Bride

Both families were very busy before the wedding. The wedding was to take place in the yard of our house at the suggestion of my father and mother.

"I'm going to invite everyone to Anna's wedding."

My mother in particular had been saying this to me seven before I married. After a disappointing marriage between Brian and Sua, my parents planned to invite friends, Father's and Brian's business associates, and acquaintances from the village, to have an outdoor wedding in our yard. Brian's uninvited wedding ceremony left a lingering sadness in our parents' hearts, but I couldn't bear to tell my parents the reason I heard from Brian.

Michael's parents decorated the house on the banks of the Niagara River that they would give to Michael when he got married. And my parents-in-law said they would call a chef on our wedding day to serve guests. Wine and champagne from both families were prepared in abundance for the reception. The parents of both families were close friends because they were doing business in the same industry and living in the same neighborhood, and the locals were guests.

Most of all, I was happy that Brian congratulated me. I am my parents' daughter, Brian's older sister, and I am now married to Michael. No matter how passionately we wanted each other to become one, it was just a passing wind in front of a stronger and stronger relationship. No one knew that I would have a relationship with such a strange person in such a close place. Brian and I were now aware of the path of that relationship.

Each of us went our own way.

The wedding in early June was grand and beautiful. The early summer, which called for a full-fledged summer, was equally abundant. In the garden, the multicolored roses that my mother and I had planted were in full bloom along the vines. Lake Ontario glistened with ripples in the sunshine and people on the boats celebrated us by waving their hands as sailboats hoisted their sails. The music played by the string quartet was carried by a gentle breeze from Lake Ontario and spread across the vineyards.

Like a faithful butler, the aging oak tree provided ample shade. It allowed those who did not welcome the sunlight to enjoy the cool breeze blowing across the lake, and my treasure chest, the tree house, looked down from the bosom of the oak tree.

'What you really don't know is what happens between people. Anna, who only knew Brian, is getting married to Michael!'

'She just met the heavenly relationship.'

'Happy, Anna!'

'Really, you should be happy, my Anna!'

It was a conversation between the tree house and the oak tree. They will cover their mouths and whisper, 'We'll be holding your first love and everything until this moment.'

Finally, the guests held their breath as the bride walked out holding the father's arm to the music between the seats set on both sides of the large backyard facing the lake.

I was the bride, the bride of June.

'Mom, Mamani is now the bride.'

I walked holding my father's arm and said to my real Peruvian mother, who was not in this world.

'Father, Mario, I'm getting married.'

I also announced my wedding to my real father and Mario, who were not in this world.

My mom, my dad, and my brother Mario seemed to be blessing me.

'Have a good life, Mama. Be happy, my Mamani.'

The bride of June, I put a little wave on my black hair and let it flow down one side of the neck like a wavy napkin along with the veil, and the white rose dress that my mother wore long ago was elegant.

When I set my wedding date, my mother urged me to go buy my wedding dress first, but I said that I wanted to wear my mother's wedding dress that my mother kept.

'Anna, this is a once in a lifetime wedding. Buy the most beautiful wedding dress.'

My mother said she wanted to enjoy the joy of choosing a wedding dress with me. My mother, who didn't enjoy Brian's wedding, seemed to be determined to do everything at my wedding.

'But, mother, I want to wear your wedding dress.'

I really wanted to wear my mother's old wedding dress. Wearing that dress, I wanted to live happily with Michael for a long time, just like my mother and my father do.

My mother, who knew of my subtle stubbornness and that I didn't talk nonsense, had no choice but to enjoy fixing the old dress she wore to fit my body instead of the pleasure of buying a dress.

'I was sorry I didn't make a bed cover for Anna, but let's fix the wedding dress instead. My daughter will look beautiful no matter what she wears.'

The decades-old wedding dress was being reborn as my wedding dress from my mother's hands.

The wedding dress was long gone, but today's star, the bride, wore it, so it must have looked more dignified and elegant.

Michael, who had completely shaved off his dark beard, looked like a nobleman with a bright and clear face that turned blue and dressed in a dark tuxedo. I didn't know why I used to hate Michael so much before even just for a moment during the ceremony. The past was all buried in joy.

My father, who was holding his daughter's hand, rubbed his eyes, hugged me tightly once, then passed me on to his son-in-law, Michael. I just smiled softly, but didn't open my eyes and look at Michael. Because Michael was looking at me even when I wasn't looking at him.

"Beautiful! Bride! Even if I think about it, I think I made the right choice."

It was a marvelous matchmaking when what Mrs. Gilmore had said became a reality.

The fresh and mild wind and warm sunlight from Lake Ontario in early summer that is neither too hot nor too cold, the light green trees and all kinds of roses in full bloom, today's main characters, and

the generous expressions of the guests who cannot take their eyes off them, made the best wedding ever.
Chefs with high white hats on their heads prepared food for their guests, and wine and champagne from both families were plentiful.

It was a wonderful wedding with Brian and Sua there too. With that, I, Mamani, who grew up as Anna Hills, now became Mrs. Anna Evans.

15. To Each Other

'It was so beautiful that I almost cried, Anna.'
It was what Sua said during the phone call after I went on a honeymoon.
Did Sua remember her first wedding? Sua's words, 'I was in tears,' touched my heart. It was the wedding where a woman with a stroller came into her wedding hall and said to Sua, 'He is the father of my child.'
'How would she have dealt with it?'
It was the tragedy of the wedding day that must have been too harsh for the bride. So I was even more sorry, I guessed I even broke Sua's heart.
She said on the phone, 'I think everyone in the family had let go of all their busy hands. Father stopped trying to say 'Anna!'and mother still called 'Anna!' from time to time and said, 'Why am I doing this, Anna is going and not here,'
Sua further told me that my mother covered the loneliness without me by blaming herself.
'Brian will feel emptiness too,' Sua also said. 'When we lived together, I didn't know, but after you left, the empty space left behind was so big, Anna,'
'Will Brian really feel empty?'
More than anyone else, I dared to think that he would feel lonely. We've been together since Brian was six and I was seven. He was my younger brother, my friend and my lover. It was Brian and I, who were bound by a deep and strong bond as much as a relationship with many meanings. How can we shake off our hearts just because we left each other in front of our eyes?
As I smiled, I was drawing a picture of Sua in my mind, who became

more talkative. Sua, who was always quiet, seemed to talk a lot because she was talking to her parents-in-law on behalf of me. Sua was like a friend I met late.

I couldn't reveal it to Sua, but I was sorry. Why didn't Sua know that the person Brian loved was me?

In Sua's tense marriage life, Brian's eyes and mine, and the conflict caused by the intertwining of those eyes, would have given Sua an unspeakable agony? It must have never been different from how I felt when I had to speak and smile softly even with Sua in front of my eyes. But Sua was always quiet, as if she knew nothing.

It meant that I could shed everything I had inside with tears in the snow-covered vineyards, but Sua endured it alive. It was as if everything that words could reveal had been submerged in her eyes like a deep well. So I was even more sorry.

'Thank you, Sua.'

I just wanted to say that. Thank you for embracing everything and, above all, thank you for being by my parents' side.

It seemed that mother would be most lonely. When we wake up in the morning, we talk together, drink tea together, go shopping together, plant flowers together, and cook food together.

Mother braided my hair in two halves from the day after I first came from Peru.

The reason for adoption was that I had to be with Brian, but when the two of us grew up, my mother was wary of us when we got close.

'Anna, Brian is your brother,'she said. It also meant that my mother could not give up being my mother.

'You must not forget your Peruvian parents and brother. When I experienced the pain of losing a child, it always bothered me that I pretended not to know the feelings of a father who had to send his child away. But I don't want you to be hurt because of your memories. You are going to live as my daughter. I want you to grow up to be bright and enjoy everything.'

All the memories of Peru, which I left at the age of seven, faded as they blended into the life my mother intended, but I was able to cherish the remnants of the memories with longing while playing the zamponya. It was okay to hold on to my childhood memories, but my mother didn't want me to get sick from it.

It was my mother, Ms. Joanne Hills, who always spoke neat and noble language in front of me and tried to show me a peaceful world without lack.

When mother sent me to my new home, she said, 'From now on, you have to think more of Michael than your mom and dad.'

Leaving mother's house with an oak tree bearing a tree house, the home where my body and mind grew up as a family since I was seven, while I followed Michael to our honeymoon on the Parkway, a 40-minute drive away, I was engraving my mother's words more deeply in my mind than ever before.

Now where Michael was is my home. I felt like I had come to a place where my body and mind could freely take root. This was the place for me and Michael to live together while confirming the deep bond that felt like I belonged to Michael and Michael belonged to me.

Now, as a couple, we did not have enough time to mature in a new relationship, but nevertheless, we had the dignity, responsibility, and duty to a relationship where anything is possible. Love would be a different color in the name. It will be a different color named love. It was the right to love, allowed only to me.

In that deep winter, when we had no choice but to grow our love in the car, the long-awaited summer started with our marriage and we began to enjoy summer games.

We biked and rollerbladed along the Niagara River parkway. We walked together along the river and on the river we floated our boat.

The Parkway, which Winston Churchill once poetically named “The Most Beautiful Sunday Afternoon Drive in the World,” had been a dating course for Michael and I since before we got married. And we boarded the boat.

Michael's speedboat, which he started to show that he was never weak, was a summer game he enjoyed, but I, not accustomed to speed, started cheering after experiencing a few horrors at the dizzying sense of speed.

I no longer held a zamponya in my hand. I didn't want to drown my heart in the sad and nostalgic music of the lost empire, longing for the Inca. The speed that seemed to burst with cheers, riding a bicycle that made the whole body wet as the tension evaporated with sweat, roller blades and speed boats were much more interesting to me.

My hands were quick, but I was used to being extremely quiet and slow, but I was gradually getting used to the speed. It was a certain tendency in me that I didn't know. I had a temperament within me that would soon bloom into flames. It was the other inclination that I had, that was, passion, which existed as if it had been imprisoned for a long time.

Michael ignited the passions within me one by one and tamed them in his own way. Every time I hesitated, Michael led me over and over again, finally getting me to speed up and enjoy rollerblading.

'You can do it, Anna! Me too!'

Every time I hesitated, Michael pulled me in, saying, 'Anna, don't be afraid, I'm doing it too!' When Michael guided me and made it possible for me to enjoy it. I discovered in him a disposition I didn't know about. It was an active and persistent drive. Michael could have been so liberated from alcohol, and he would have made me fall in love, who had hated him, and finally made me his wife.

"Now I know that it was fun and happy when we were together, Anna."

While biking along the parkway along the Niagara River, Michael and I sat down at a picnic table with the bikes lying on the grass. In the meantime, Michael said he rode a speedboat and rollerblade alone.

"You said you were always alone?"

It meant that Michael had no friends by his side. It broke my heart to hear that he and Brian had met at business meetings but he was alone while playing.

"It's what I wanted."

"Did you want it? Why?"

We were looking at the very slow flowing Niagara River.

"I had to isolate myself from people in order to start treatment properly, so I decided to isolate myself."

So, it was a self-selected isolation for the treatment of alcoholism. What he meant was that he had distanced himself from the gatherings where alcohol was shared for the purpose of treatment.

"My mother wanted to get rid of all the bottles of wine in our house, but to do that, we had to sell our winery first. I told my mother not to do that. After all, it was a fight with myself. There was a lot of wine in the winery and house. Wine was something I could get whenever I wanted. I was living in a wine town.

"I wanted to beat myself so that I couldn't get my hands on it even with the wine in front of me. I wanted to work hard. So one day I ran and rode alone, another day I rollerbladed alone, and the next day I rode a bike, completely isolating me from people and from alcohol."

"How hard it must have been, alone!"

"It was so hard that I wanted to give up. All my friends work hard, get married, have children, and live a life appropriate for their age, but when I fell into a sense of shame that my life was far behind, I wanted to throw myself into a bottle of wine again."

I quit smoking then too, Michael said.

"But in my head, a cold thought followed me that if I couldn't do this, my life wouldn't be possible. I haven't lived my life properly yet, but if I don't have my life, isn't it too unfair? I was really scared back then. I wanted to lean on someone. 'It's okay Michael, you can do it,'must have been what I wanted to hear."

"Oh, Michael!"

It felt like my heart was breaking. It meant that Michael was desperately reaching out to someone when I had an antagonism in my childhood memories. I was sorry, as if I had shrugged off his hand that reached out to me.

"My parents cried and begged, 'You can do it, Michael,' and encouraged me, but when I turned away from my parents and became completely alone, I started to miss those words. One day, a thought suddenly occurred to me, and now is the time when I need my will. When I'm completely alone, that's when I do it. So I changed my mind. Let's enjoy what I have to do anyway. As I steered through the water on the speedboat, I thought that I was not weak, and as I rode the rollerblades, I was determined that I would never fall again. I thought that I would work hard after riding a bicycle or running alone, and I would meet a good person I want to walk with when I walk alone. And I think a lot about my family, which I've never had when I was drunk. I also suffered because of my awkward words and actions, but I wondered how much harder it must have been for my parents. When I think about it like that, I keep thinking of people who must have suffered because of me, and Brian and Anna were among them."

"Me too?"

It was Michael's confession that I never unexpected.

"Yeah, thinking about Anna was painful in itself. It took me too long

to regret what I did to a child who would have had a hard time in an unfamiliar place where she couldn't speak at such a young age, but by that time it was already too late.
There were times when I was riding a bike, walking, or running by myself, wondering if I might meet Anna. I had to say I'm sorry, but I didn't know how we never met in the same neighborhood."
When I was afraid that I might meet by chance, Michael was expecting to meet me by chance.

"My mother told me whenever she went to a wives'gathering, 'today Anna from the Hills house came with her mother'. There was also a time when I thought about going to the wives' meeting as an excuse for driving. But when I heard what Mrs. Gilmore had said from my mother, I was glad inside that I had finally got my chance to apologize, but it was not easy to call you, I was afraid that you would reject my call."

I didn't think about it often, but when I still had an antipathy for Michael in my heart, Michael looked back on his own actions, even his actions when he was young and immature, regretting and looking for an opportunity to apologize to me.

"It was the most, most serious time of my life when I thought about myself and my relationships with others. And then I started to stop drinking alcohol. I put wine in front of me and didn't touch it, so my father, who was watching me, told me to try a winery business."

"So, you mean, your Father trusted you"

"Yes, my father entrusted me with alcohol. My father risked his child's life and his own business. I wanted to do it a little differently. So I had to do market research, research the relationship between wine and food, people's preferences, and take into account the characteristics of the neighborhood."

I kissed Michael on the cheek. It was because Michael was so wonderful in my mind. Michael looked at me with a happy expression on his face and kissed me.

"I did it once by myself, but I can't do it twice. I found it happiest to be with Anna and having fun together."

"I will never leave you alone again, Michael."
I really am, I wasn't going to leave him alone. That's why we became a couple.

"Anna, there are so many things I want to do with you, there are so many things I want to do with you when our children are born. I will try them all one by one."

Who would have thought that a conversation like this would come and go between Michael and me? Michael and I, who seemed unlikely to see each other again while accumulating only bad memories, became the most precious people to each other. And we have more to look forward to, our children. It was our children who would share what Michael had planned.

16. Her, Sua

"I miss you, Anna."
When Sua, who does not reveal her feelings well, said on the phone, 'I miss you,'I had a different thought. Did she ever have a hard time?, So does she have anything to say to me?
My mother said, 'Call Sua often, my dear', and she even gently urged me to call her.

"I am busy following Ian these days."
Sua talked about Ian while eating and drinking tea. Then, Sua smiled happily. It was a smile that only the mother of a child could put on. Now, Ian was a very busy baby to whom Sua couldn't take her eyes off even for a moment. He walked like running, looking only in front of him.

I was very envious of Sua, a mother who smiles with satisfaction. I also wanted to give birth to a baby and follow the baby who walks like running, looking forward, but I didn't have any pregnancy status yet.

"Anna, I have something I want to tell you."
Sua, who had only talked about Ian until the meal was over, put the teacup in front of her and suddenly hesitated.

"I thought a lot about whether it was okay to say it or not."
She meant that the reason she wanted to see me was because she had something to say.

"I want to hear."
I looked at Sua and smiled. I don't know what she means, but I wanted to make it easy for Sua to speak.
She lowered her eyes for a moment, bit her lip, seemed to think, and then began to speak.

"When Brian said he had an unfulfilled love, I wondered who that woman was. I was really curious back then. But the day Brian was

angry because of Michael, I knew."
Sua blew a bomb on me out of nowhere. That day, Sua finally found out why Brian was suddenly angry when mother told us about what Mrs. Gilmore said at a meeting that day. So, though she knew everything, she pretended not to know.

'So, she got up from her seat first and left!'

I managed to clear my mind and remembered what happened that day. Because of my personal affairs, Brian was rude to mother, and it was a dangerous word and behavior that could lead to the misunderstanding that he still had not erased me from his heart. Moreover, it was in front of Sua.

Now, Sua mentioned the relationship between me and Brian so belatedly.

It was as if Sua was scolding me by saying, 'How could you love my husband, your brother?'I didn't know what to do with myself. At the same time, I was thinking about what Sua, who was living a good life with a family, was making me uncomfortable by suddenly bringing up the past with Brian and me. Brian said he wanted to put Sua at ease. Isn't that how it works? Or does it mean that Sua still doesn't know Brian's heart? So does that mean she's suspicious of me? The timing was not right to doubt me like that. Because I already became Michael's wife and I only care about Michael.

"Before I met Brian, I knew a man."

Sua threw another bomb of unexpected words. It seemed that Sua was determined to surprise me today.

"I was at my wedding with him, and suddenly a woman with a stroller showed up and said, 'That's my baby's dad."

I was bewildered as to why Sua was doing this today, but she was talking about her wedding, which she wanted to forget, as if she were talking to someone else. It was at Sua's own wedding, which I heard from Brian before my wedding. I had no idea what she was trying to say to me, or why Sua herself was telling me about the harsh wedding scene that had nothing to do with me. Sua has been silent until now for the parents who were so sad because they did not know the reason for not attending their son's wedding.

"I was a bride, and a woman and a baby I didn't know suddenly appeared and messed up my wedding."

But once she started talking, she didn't seem to want to stop. It was an unconventional expression of what Sua, who usually talks a little, showed.

"People were screaming and the ceremony stopped. I was shivering in front of the ceremony without doing this or that with a veil on, and the woman said again, 'Don't do that to my baby, please!' Obviously she was looking at me. It was only then that I came to my senses. It wasn't that they were messing with my wedding, but it was I who was taking her husband and her baby's dad away from them."

Sua spoke calmly as if it was someone else's business, but tears welled up in Sua's eyes, like a deep well. However, I still couldn't figure out why Sua was scratching her heart so much and revealing to me all her inner feelings that I couldn't even understand.

"I felt sorry for Anna. It was as if I was standing in front of Anna in that veil again."

"...?

What was Sua talking about now?

That moment when Brian got angry reminded Sua of that moment at her wedding where she took the woman's husband and her baby's father from the women and the baby.

'Oh, my God! Sua could have thought like this!'

I was so embarrassed. It was so embarrassing that I couldn't even open my mouth.

In order to say 'I'm sorry', Sua exposed the moment of her wedding that would have been a shame, but I still couldn't even sympathize with Sua's 'I'm sorry'. Because I have never lost my love to anyone. When I ran into the boundary of a family relationship that had strong roots, I just chose a different color of love for siblings that was originally established. The boundaries my parents set were so strong that Brian didn't know, but at least I already knew that I could never cross the line. It meant that I was aware of the stark reality of my position being different from Brian. Even so, it was not Sua's fault because the terrible heartache I had to suffer was the price I had to pay for falling in love with an impossible love.

"I think I must have made it difficult for you as I looked at you

every day."
Sua confessed again.
'Every day in front of my eyes...'
Sua knew my position. In front of Sua and Brian, I had to talk and laugh every day as if nothing had happened. And it was also the feeling I felt for Sua. She was talking about the pain Sua would have suffered because of me.

Sua broke the jar of memories she had buried deep in front of me and poured out all the harsh memories she never wanted to look back on. What should I say? What should I say about my first love, which was Sua's love? According to Soo-a's method, which was exposed even while suffering the pain of breaking, I have to reveal everything from the time I was seven years old, but should I do the same?
I didn't want to. The thing that Sua and I never wished for would be like that, but inevitably happened, the thing now I buried in my heart, I didn't want to bring it out in front of Sua and say it again, no, I couldn't.
That first love that was everything to a child from a young age until she became an adult, no matter how much it is Sua's love now, that long time of my first love was mine. I wanted to treat my first love my way. Burying the past in me as the past was a courtesy to my first love and my way of dealing with my past.
Now Sua and I each have Brian and Michael, and at this point in time when we can only see each other's love, I thought that we didn't need any other words other than love in front of us.

I quietly took Sua's hand, hoping she would understand the meaning of my silence. Because silence is itself a silent language that takes the place of many words.

17. Couple

The Niagara River in front of my house sparkling with scales was like a starry night sky. It was the water flowing into Lake Ontario in front of my mother's house. Lake Erie is less than 20 minutes away from my house, and my mother's house on the shores of Lake Ontario is about 40 minutes away.

As the water of Lake Erie passes through the Peace Bridge connected to the United States, its name is changed to the Niagara River, and it flows in front of the house as if it were staying sleepy. Then it meets a cliff and becomes a waterfall. The flow of water falls to the bottom, circling and foaming, then again meeting whirlpools and canyons, and finally reaches the sea-like lake, Ontario. It resembles a life that is sometimes rough like waterfalls and rapids, and sometimes sleepy and quiet.

When Michael goes to work, sometimes I leave the house on my bike. It's an outing to Niagara Falls or to Lake Erie.
At the waterfall, a huge stream of water falls vertically day and night. The water flows peacefully, but when it suddenly falls off a cliff, it seems to slow down around without energy. It is the same image of me as a child when I came to an unfamiliar land with my roots buried in the land of Peru, and was swayed by different languages, conflicts with different ideas, and different customs and cultures.

The stream, which had been curled up as if dead, began to move, wiping away the bubbles as time passed, and the water, which was moving very slowly, reunited with each other in front of the increasingly narrow river, accelerating the flow. Then soon, when it meets a canyon, it flows like a running horse with its mane and finally arrives at the lake of the sea, Ontario.

Even though it started flowing from a stream, the water that reached Ontario is now a lake with many types of fish. Lake Ontario, which is always quiet even after embracing all its tributaries, is the mother of rivers, where they can relax and rest before the water goes to the sea and settles down.

There were times when I felt Ontario from my mother.
This is because the mother's arms are always generous like Ontario, which embraces rivers of all kinds and numerous kinds of fish.
As a wife and best friend to my father, she raised me as the same child as Brian. Even though my mother suffered from the abduction of her only son, Brian, she was the one who firmly defended the family more than anyone else in the family. That was why, above all, when family members encountered obstacles in their lives, and when it was difficult to stand up, they first looked to their mother. My mother was Ontario, and Ontario was my mother.

Lake Ontario is also the sky lake of Peru, Titicaca to me. At the edge of the lake, which is made up of water flowing down from the melting ice and snow of the Andean Mountains, flocks of birds soared among the thick reeds. Peruvians believe that the Inca civilization began at Lake Titicaca.
Ontario, where I came from Titicaca when I was seven, has as many different languages, different thoughts, and different cultures as the lakes contain as many kinds of fish, but now that I am a local, Ontario is more familiar and friendlier than Titicaca.
Looking back, even though I had encountered many unfamiliar things every day until I could enjoy the peace on the shores of Lake Ontario, I was able to get used to it one by one while living as a family with my mother, father, and Brian.
Now, years have passed and Michael and I have created a world called a separate family, and many more years have passed.

My mother-in-law and father-in-law, who became my new family because of Michael, are warm and loving people just like my mother and father. My mother-in-law, Mrs. Evans, whom I have become acquainted with at wives' gatherings when I accompanied my mother occasionally, treated me like her daughter in a family without a daughter.

'Anna, Michael became a new person after meeting you.'
My parents-in-law believed that it was because I was by his side that Michael was abstaining from alcohol and focused on running a winery and restaurant. But my thoughts were different. Michael had already become a new person before he met me.
It was because Michael had decided on himself the last course of treatment and finally overcame the process himself. After soberly grasping his own weakness, he fought with himself to overcome it. It was Michael's will. But whenever my parents-in-law said about it, I felt a deep bond as a member of the Evans family. It was because my parents-in-law's words meant that they believed in me. Now, if Michael and I had a child, there would be no more hope, but for some reason there was no news of pregnancy.

Even if it wasn't for my parents-in-law's silent waiting, the more time passed, the more anxious I became. Although time has passed for Brian and Sua's son Ian to go to school, and Sua had a second child, a daughter, I did not show any signs of pregnancy. I really wanted to have a baby and be hugged by both families and Michael. Above all, I wanted to please my parents-in-law who said, 'Michael has become a new person after meeting you', and I wanted to satisfy my mother, who said, 'I think my grandson completes me. This feeling is good.'
But there was no news of pregnancy, and when Michael went to a meeting of members doing the same business, he stopped talking at some point. I never said it was because of the child, but that was how I interpreted Michael's feelings.

Michael and Brian were quite motivated to compete in good faith in winery and farm management. The two were actively expanding their business by converting their parents' farms and wineries into modern facilities and pioneering overseas markets.
Michael's winery and restaurant business, which started after researching the preferences of tourists visiting famous wine regions, went well. At least in that world, Michael was confident, and his outspoken management style and trend-setting consumer demands matched.

Michael's aggressive business management policy, 'Different', may also have the meaning of discrimination that Michael was conscious

of Brian.
For Michael, Brian was the one who caused rivalry, quarrels, and envy long before he became brother-in-law, but Brian was the one who bothered him in every case, far from the exhilaration of suppression. In particular, the rivalry and envy towards Brian who tried to protect me would remain in the bottom of his chest even now as an adult. I knew that Michael wanted to overcome the chronic slump with his business success and his image as a strong protector. But, there was one thing that made Michael wither. A child.

Michael, who could not participate in the conversation when his friends were talking about their growing children at a friends meeting, began to feel alienated with a depressed mood. He was waiting for a child as much as I was. When a child was born, there were so many things that he wanted to do with his child. Unable to engage in a common conversation with his friends, Michael might have started holding a glass of wine instead.
Irritability arose within me as well. When Sua had her second child, Rachel, I was involuntarily comparing myself to Sua, and it felt no different than Michael competing with Brian. The more I compared, the more shabby I felt as if I would never be able to walk side by side with them again, who were already far ahead. So I understood Michael. Unable to overcome my nervousness, I also started drinking wine.

"Brian asked how you are. Is Anna happy?"
Today, Michael seemed to have been drinking wine at the meeting. I was worried that one drink would become two and that the drinking would increase again. But I couldn't say, 'No wine, Michael.' Michael himself knew better that moderation was required.
"But Anna, why does that make me feel weird? Why is Brian asking about your happiness?"
I felt a thorn in Michael's slightly drunken words. So I didn't answer right away.
"Aren't you happy with me?"
It was as if Michael's harsh words were pushing me into a corner.
"He must have wanted to know how his sister was doing."I used the word 'sister' intentionally. But why did Brian ask about my happiness? Did he think I might not be happy? Was he starting to worry about me because Michael started holding a glass of wine at a meeting? A

long time ago, Brian said in front of his parents again, 'Michael, he's an alcoholic, and it's not easy to fix'.

"But why did his question bother me? I could ask Brian about Sua's well-being, but I couldn't ask about her happiness, right?"

Michael was obsessed with those words too. The reason he was obsessed with words that could be taken over was probably drunkenness. It seemed that old sediments that had been sinking deep in his heart were floating in Michael's voice.

Michael's expression, speaking as if pushing me, recalled memories of my childhood when my whole body trembled even when my eyes met young Michael. It was a memory that I never wanted to look back on as I had to sit there and bear it.

Where does the longing for each other go, and Michael doubts me, and I am reminded of childhood memories that I do not want to look back on? Is this because of the time that passed between the two of us, which dulled our earnest feelings, or is it because of the child we do not have? Whatever the reason, it was heartbreaking.

Without further ado, I left Michael and filled the glass with wine. I was in the process of increasing my drinking.

"Are you drinking?"

Michael, who didn't know that I had given up on the occasional drink at mealtime with family members, thought I hated wine.

"Yes."

"If you drink, I drink too,"was a rather aggressive response. It was also my own way of conveying my intentions silently to Michael, who was increasing his drinking, 'You should cut down on drinking, okay?' And then I drank the wine.

"Anna!"

Michael widened his eyes.

"Wine is everywhere."

No matter how Brian felt when he said those words to me, the words shouldn't act as this kind of distrust between Michael and me.

It was because Brian and I had already not allowed each other's minds as brother and sister.

However, it was very sad that Michael, no matter how drunk he was, was making a fuss with such a prank voice. I said as I filled the glass again.

"Michael, I only know you. Brian? Yes, he is my brother I love. So

what's he up to? Why are you arguing with me about the feelings you felt? If it's between you and Brian, shouldn't the two of us solve it?"
Then I gulped down again. Michael looked at me blankly. I looked into his eyes as if I was shooting him, and my reckless appearance made Michael seem dumb.
It must have been a reaction he had never seen before.
"Anna!"
Then Michael called my name and took the wine glass from my hand that I was about to bring back to my mouth. For a moment, my strength that had been stretched out in Michael's hand subsided.
With the wine glass taken, I looked at Michael for a long time. My eyes looking at Michael must have contained resentment, anger, and worries: 'If you start drinking again, you'll have a hard time again.'
But Michael closed his eyes for a moment as if dazzled by those eyes.
And suddenly he grabbed my waist with his thick arms. It was a very fleeting thing.
"Anna!"
And we fell on the sofa. It was never meant to create such an atmosphere.
We fell on the sofa.
His breathing was already rough and his hands were urgent. I made no objections. I left this incomprehensible reaction, in which the desire, which had subsided as if dead, began to wriggle in spite of still being sad.
However, Michael's behavior, which started to burn as he wanted to after he had doubts, suddenly awakened the memories of many childhood days when he made fun of me. That was the time when Michael played me with all sorts of mischievous words and made fun of me.
At that time, why did I cover my face and sit down and not say a word, despite my familiar language, Quechua? Why, I was so embarrassed by Michael's language that I didn't understand, that I floundered at what I could have defended.
I should have been able to suppress Michael's frivolous language and behavior with my own language, so that he would never be rude again.
However, regrets that I couldn't do at that time were wriggling within me now. And it was to stimulate my willpower that had been hidden as if it was not there.

All of his actions were already covered by a single word, 'We were all young back then.' But at this moment, a thought like anger suddenly came to my mind, 'Michael, if you get mad at me now with something that's not a big deal, I'll have no choice but to show you my disposition.'
It was like a warning to Michael to never again harass me in his own way, never again to scratch himself and me and doubts that would damage our relationship according to his mood.
I put the brakes on his relentless hand and pushed his hot lips away. Michael frowned at my gesture of refusal, which he had never seen before.
He looked at me.
I woke up.
Then I filled the glass again and took a sip.
"What are you doing, Anna!"
"Michael, you still treat me like I was when I was a kid, and now you doubt me. Do you want to do it again?"
I took off my blouse, half loose from Michael's hands. And I untied the bra that was tightening my chest and threw it away. My two breasts, which had been hidden, sprung out like springs, and stood upright in front of Michael.
Michael stepped back. His eyes widened. It was a look that had lost all the alcohol.
"I want to drink more."
I reached over the table again and grabbed Jean's waist. and filled the cup.
"Anna!"
Michael took the cup from my hand again. And he hugged my shoulder.
"I'm sorry, don't do this. I was wrong."
His arms gripped me.
"I understand, Anna. I'm sorry for making you do this.'
Michael kept talking while holding me.
'You got it?'
My angry heart stayed on the word, 'understand' rather than 'wrong' or 'sorry'.
I wanted to believe Michael's words, but I couldn't say or do any more. It wasn't because of his strength that imprisoned me, but because

of his word 'I got it'. There was nothing more for me to add if he understood the meaning of my actions.
When I thought about it, Michael and I had a relationship in which we flirted with each other's words to confirm each other's feelings, but eventually understood each other as to why they were doing this.
That's right.
It was the couple.

18. Oh, Mother

Ahead of the children's summer vacation, Brian and Sua decided to take their two children to Korea. My mother encouraged Sua, who had not been able to go to her family for a long time.

'Sua, if you go to Korea this time, invite your parents here in Canada. Your parents will also want to see how you live.'

Thanks to her mother-in-law's gratitude, Sua was able to invite her parents to Canada. Sua couldn't cheer like a child, but she only laughed.

My mother and father taught grandchildren what to do when they meet grandfather and grandmother on their mother's side in Korea. Ian, studying about his mother's country, Korea, on the internet, fueled his calm excitement before he even left for Korea.

Many years have passed since Sua came here, but I was very envious that Sua had a family she could visit. Even if I couldn't go often, it must have been a strength and comfort to have someone somewhere I could visit.

I was thinking of my Peruvian father and mother, and my brother Mario, who were no longer in this world. It hurts the more I think about how everyone left and left me alone. Mom, Dad, and brother seemed to have left me so that I could forget everything and live in a new family and a new house. If so, it was clear that my mother, father, and older brother had never thought of the loss within me, as there is no one that I can meet when I return to my hometown.

As I looked at Sua, who was busy with shopping and packing ahead of visiting her mother's home in Korea, I felt even more lonely.

Then I suddenly thought of my father and my mother here.

The problem has always been with me. This house where my parents live is my own home, and even though I received so much love, I could not have my father and mother in the place of my real parents in Peru. I made a promise to see my parents every day while the Brian family was in Korea. It would have been a month, but it would be unbearable for parents to keep quiet in an empty house with no children.

Finally, after the family of four left for Korea with large luggage, I went to my mother's home every day to have lunch or drink tea with my mother and father and returned to my house.

"The four of us left at once, so this place is really empty, Anna. When does a month pass?"

They have just left and my mother is already waiting for Brian's family.

"Joanne, do you want to play with me? Shall we go on a trip somewhere?"

Father tried to calm mother, pretending it was okay.

"It's hard to go out in the heat, Tom. Let's just cool off at home."

After all, my mother and father didn't travel, and I saw them during the daytime when Michael was at work. And sometimes I climbed up the tree house and played zamponya.

"Why doesn't Diego go there once?"

It had been a while since Diego, who was doing all the housework, no longer came from Mexico, and my mother, who suddenly became idle, waited for Diego who had left a long time ago.

"How easy is it to write a novel? Diego said he brought a book with him, so let's wait, Joan."

"Writing a novel is very difficult. Diego said he brought a book with him, so let's wait, Joan."

"How difficult would it be to have people compare writing to labor pains? I think vineyards would be easier."

Sometimes when my mother was holding a glass of wine with her family, she said, 'Of all fruit farming, there is no sensitive farm that requires as many hands as grape farming, but a glass of wine will compensate for the tedious process.'

Father, who gave Ian a sense of responsibility as he looked at the vineyard and said to Ian, 'Look, Ian, that farm, you will become the owner of that farm,'seemed to be waiting for Diego for nothing.

Perhaps my father, who stood with his growing grandson and instilled a sense of ownership, might be more lonely than my mother for the time being.

Father now entrusted most of the work to Brian, running the farm and winery.
These days, when they meet friends in the same industry, they spend a very slow and quiet day talking to each other about what they can do to help young people in their business.
'I've been working all my life, Brian. I also want to enjoy life with your mother.'
This was what my father said when he left the winery and farm work to Brian.
My mother still attended the wives' gatherings once a month, and on the day of the meetings, my mother was particularly concerned with her attire and hairdo.
The mother took care of her appearance even more considering the face of Evans, who is now an in-law, and each other. She was still beautiful.
"I have to go to the meeting tomorrow. Anna, you rest."
When I visited my parents yesterday, my mother's voice was like a leaf fluttering in the wind.
"Then what do I do?"
When my mother said that she had an appointment, my father acted like a child for nothing.
"Would you like to go to the meeting with me, Tom?"
My father also waved at my mother's words.
"Would you like to have lunch with me, Dad?"
"No, Anna. I'm actually a busy person."
At my father's words, my mother and I looked at each other and laughed, and my father laughed along with it.

Since I didn't have to go to my parents' house, I decided to spend the day relaxing at home after Michael went to work.
The midsummer sun was scorching hot before it even reached the top of its head. Outside the window, people enjoying the heat on the Niagara River have already started to float boats and split the water. The Niagara River, which had been quiet without a single wind, twisted and foamed as the boat passed by. No matter how hot it is in summer, it is powerless in front of the river.
I fell into a nap while reading a book, thinking that it would be better to stay at home, as my mother said, unless I go out to the river or the sea in the heat like today. After sleeping for so long, I woke up to the

sound of a sudden phone call.
"The police. Are you Anna Evans?"
The other party was a man with a very business-like but polite voice.

The word 'police' seemed to cool my mind, which had been hazy from taking a nap. Why was my head so surprised at the word 'police' even though I didn't do anything wrong?
It was probably because the moment I heard the word 'Police', an incident occurred to me that my brother Mario was caught one day by the oncoming police and left handcuffed before my eyes. When I was a child, before I came here with my step parents.
What's going on with the police now without that Mario? For a moment I was thinking of Michael again, could he have had an accident with him while he was drinking? I thought.
Now was not the time for Michael to get close to alcohol, but nonetheless, no other possibility came to mind in my anxious mind. I felt shocked and disoriented. He was the one who said he could never go back to that terrible time of treatment.
"What's going on?"
I asked as calmly as possible.
"Are you Joanne Hills' daughter?"
"Why mother? What's wrong with my mother?"
It was then that I remembered what my mother said when I visited my mother's house yesterday, 'There is a meeting of friends today', and then my mother's driving accident. Yesterday my mother obviously said, 'Anna, we're going to have lunch a little farther away this time, on the side of the waterfall.'
The restaurant near the waterfall was not far from my house.
"Your mother is looking for you."
The reason my mother was looking for me through the police, that obviously meant something had happened to her and I drove straight to the place where she was.
My mother's car was parked on the side of the road near Niagara Falls, and she was in the car. A police officer was talking to my mother outside.
"Mother!"
"Oh, Anna, Anna!"
As soon as mother saw me, she held my hand and cried.
"Mother, it's okay, it's okay."

I hugged my crying mother's shoulder. My mother, who must have been surprised by something, was trembling.
"Was my mother hurt?"
I turned around and asked the police officer.
"No, I think there has been some confusion."
Memories, chaos? It was the first time I heard it. So, the policeman said that my mother, who must have been driving, had a problem with her memory and forgot the way home. So while standing in one place for a long time, it was noticed by the police, who thought it strange.
I couldn't understand why my mother had lost her way home.

I went home with my mother. For thirty minutes or so on the way home, my mother said nothing. I didn't ask her anything so she could put her mind at ease.
When I got home, I laid my mother down and prepared hot tea even on a hot day.
"I am lost, Anna."
There was fear in her eyes.
"It's a familiar road, isn't it, mother?"
I said as I pulled up a chair next to my mother's chair and sat down.
"It's a familiar road. It's a road I'll never lose. But from the restaurant to the waterfall, the road disappeared."
So, my mother said, she was standing, not knowing where to go.
"What happened to me, Anna? How could I not know the way back home from the waterfall I have passed my whole life?"
My mother held my hand tightly with one hand. Mother shook her hand.
"Right now, I can picture in my head how to get home from the waterfall, but why did I do that?"
Really, why didn't my mother remember the way at that time? How could the road to home have disappeared from her memory, on the road she traveled all her life? Even if my mother had her memories gone from her head for a moment, I didn't want to think that my mother might have senile amnesia. The disease that the elderly suffer most was very scary.
'Is it because of Brian who went to Korea?'
I managed to recall my mother, who had been anxious a few years ago to imagine that Brian might not return from Korea. Furthermore, in her consciousness, the memory of the loss of young Brian was lurking.

Coincidentally, Brian is now leaving with Sua and his two children. Since his family was not here now, did the wounds of loss in my mother's consciousness appear to get lost?

"Do you miss the Brian family, mother?"

Knowing my mother's feelings, I asked implicitly.

"I feel anxious when Brian is not in front of me."

So it meant that Brian's absence was still acting as a factor that made mother anxious. The anxiety that had been built up in my mother for a long time might have turned out to be lost on the way back home. To my mother, the house and Brian were the most precious things.

"Brian always came home. Because parents are there."

"Yes, Brian was back home. Even when he was five years younger, he called his mother on the street that night."

My mother nodded her head and slowly closed her eyes as if she couldn't bear the weight of her eyelids. I could imagine how embarrassed she must have been and how frightened she must have been because of the lost road while driving.

Afraid of my mother's unfamiliar symptoms, I fell to my mother's chest, who was sleeping soundly, and cried.

My mother, Mrs. Joanne Hills.

My mother was the one who, after marrying my father, helped my father expand his business from a small vineyard to a large farm and winery.

My mother knew what the workers were supposed to do with the seasons, and how the weather affected the vineyards, and she knew the time of harvest. She even knew how to compare writing novels with the sensitive vine farms.

My mother knew how to treat workers from distant lands year after year, and she was wise enough to know how the exchange of conversations over meals and tea at wives' gatherings would affect my father's wine business. Whenever my father was weary and shaken by running a big business that would never have been simple, she was the one who walked closest to him.

She was my mother to me because she adopted me as her daughter when I was young, who had lost her real mother early.

When Brian and I crossed the border between siblings and tried to break that boundary, my mother made our relationship clear. She was the mother who kept her family in order even though she suffered the pain of having to send her child away again with severe resentment.

I grew up listening to my mother's words that contained her character, and I grew up in her by seeing the way my mother showed me. So, if I had a good disposition in me, it would be the influence of her life that she showed and told me.

My heart ached to see my mother, who walked with the family members whenever they were having a hard time, crying in bewilderment after losing the way you had to go, and falling asleep exhausted.

19. And Chaos

For several days, I was drowsy and unmotivated. After Michael left for work, I went back to bed and lay down. It was like a cold that came in late summer.

I got out of the bed to drink hot tea and suddenly the spicy chili my mother made came to my mind. It was a thick stew of minced meat, vegetables, red kidney beans, and chili. Eating a bowl of chili that was not greasy seemed to give me energy. I left the house right away and went to Tim Hortons. I wanted to refresh my head with coffee, and most of all, I wanted to eat chili.

It may not taste the same as the one my mother made, but the hot chili in front of me seemed to give me energy even before I tasted it. I could eat the whole bowl at once. I was in a hurry, so I took a spoonful and put it in my mouth.

".?"

The moment I put the chili in my mouth, which I was so desperate for, I choked up and something popped up inside me. It was a symptom I had never experienced before. I took another spoonful and put it in my mouth. Again, I choked up in my stomach and a lump came from inside me.

'...!'

All of a sudden, my head lit up as if a lot of five-colored egg bulbs were turned on at once, like a Christmas light.

A shiver went up to my toes, and it seemed as if the peripheral nerves, which had been sluggish, were beating all at once. My heart was so full that it was hard to even breathe. Though nothing was certain, my thoughts kept leaning in one direction.

It was the symptom that I had heard countless times, waited for a long time, but never happened, so I was disappointed and exhausted and was about to give up. I calmed down by pressing my chest gently.

'Mom!'

In that circumstance, I called neither Michael nor my mother, but the real my mother from Peru, who passed away while giving birth. My word was Quechua.

Tears spilled out. Through the strong sunlight and the sea-like Lake Titicaca and the rough reed forest, the rough face of my real mother, who was tormented by the wind, passed faintly. It was my real mother who sat with her young daughter, Mamani, like an old bag, selling jewelry she had made all night. I also remembered her blood-soaked bottom and my mother's distorted face covered in tears. She was a mother who had never escaped from a life of poverty and hardship.

'Mom, I think I'm going to be a mother.'

I tried to calm it down, but tears kept pouring down. I missed my real mother, whom I had forgotten at my young age because I was living in an unfamiliar country with my new family. It was the first time that my heart had been inclined to one side so much over something that was not certain.

'Michael!'

I thought of calling Michael, but I changed my mind. I decided to let him know after a more accurate diagnosis. So I bought a pregnancy tester at the pharmacy.

"Oh, God!"

Two red lines were clear. It was the first announcement of its existence with two red lines. I thought I'd like anything red, or two parallel lines in the future. My baby was a precious baby who wanted chili but refused to eat it.

I wanted to enjoy this profound feeling of happiness just for one night, alone with the baby. It was a life that came after nine years. I wanted to have a quiet conversation with the baby, saying, 'Mom was tired of waiting for you, but now baby, you are making me the happiest.' Then I changed my mind. Although Michael didn't say anything about waiting for the baby, he was eagerly waiting for the baby too. I thought I should give Michael my happiness as a beautiful gift when he returns home. I was going to show the two bright red lines of the diagnostic machine right in front of Michael. My mind went this way and that, and I couldn't get it to go.

Around these times, Michael was increasing his drinking every time he went to the meeting. He's going to be a dad soon, so he won't be doing that anymore. Of course, Michael will make a decision again. He was a person who overcame the difficult treatment. And he was the one who made me turn my hatred heart to love.

The baby wanted it, so I enjoyed the drowsy symptoms. Surely, my baby wants good ideas, I imagined flowers and a tree house. I thought of the sailboats on Lake Ontario, the black grapes ripening on the vineyards, and then I remembered what my mother told us when Sua had a baby.
Mother said, 'I liked being a grandmother, but it was also a bit sad, but when I think about it again, it was a very happy thing. It felt like my grandson was perfecting me.'
'My baby, you are making Mom and Dad complete as parents too.'
It was a life that would make my father-in-law and mother-in-law, my mother and father happy once again as grandfathers and grandmothers to enjoy the joy of completion.
What came to my mind at that moment was how the whole family made Sua happy when she had Ian. There were now two families to me, my in-laws and my parents. It was overwhelming just thinking about how happy the two family members would be.

Michael was late today. I could tell him over the phone, but I wanted to share this heartwarming feeling of happiness face to face. I waited nine years, so this was nothing. I fell asleep while waiting for Michael, enjoying the bliss of the first meeting with the baby. I put the diagnostic device with two bright red lines on the table, which I wanted to show Michael.
I heard the doorbell ring in my sleep. If it were Michael, he would have opened it himself, but the doorbell rang, so I got up and went to the front door.
"Brian!"
Brian was outside the front door, holding Michael's shoulders.
"Anna!"
Never once had Michael entered the house with Brian. Michael leaned on Brian's shoulder.
"He got a little drunk."
It must have been the words of a younger brother who thought about

his older sister who might be worried about her drunken husband. Maybe that was not what it meant. Rather, on the contrary, it might be a resentment, 'That's why I was so against it.'

“I have to drive instead, Anna.”
While supporting Michael, Brian spoke like an excuse. I said to him with my eyes, 'I'm sorry Brian, for making you worry.'
“Thank you, Brian.”
But no matter how much Brian is my little brother, I didn't want to show him this ugly side of Michael. I wanted to show him only a happy and peaceful image that would dispel all of his worries.

Suddenly I remembered why I had been waiting for Michael. I wanted to let him know of the happiness that overflows in me as we face each other. But Michael was not sober, and Brian was standing in front of him. I wanted to tell Brian before he left the house. 'Brian, I have a baby.'
Brian will certainly congratulate me with all his heart. But again I suppressed my thoughts. I wanted to let Michael know this good news more than anyone else. Michael had to know first.

“Are you okay alone?”
Brian said as he left the room after putting Michael on the bed. I could read Brian's thoughts just by the sound of his words and his eyes. It was Brian who wanted to say, 'Anna, let's go home with me,'
“It’s okay, Brian. Don't tell mother, okay?"
Even in those circumstances, I didn't want my mother to know. It was clear that she would be worried about Michael, who would start drinking again.
I didn't want Michael to be the object of my family's worries. Moreover, when the Brian family was in Korea, my mother was in a very bad mood after she got lost while driving.
After Brian returned from Korea, we got together to discuss mother's symptoms, and then took her to see a doctor.
The doctor who did the memory test told her to return her driver's license, saying, 'For the safety of yourself and others, you should stop driving.'
‘I can still drive!’
At the doctor's advice, mother begged and eventually burst into tears.

The fact that she could no longer drive a car after returning the driver's license that she had acquired when she was young, must have been shocking and disappointing.

'I am now useless.'

That day, my mother cried a lot. And she gradually reduced her speech. I couldn't get my heavy-hearted mother to pay attention to Michael's drinking.

Brian looked at me quietly and hugged me.

Suddenly, the spring of that year, the day of tree house, passed by in my mind.

The wind blowing along Lake Ontario was sweet, and I was blowing the zamponya, while smelling the fishy smell of the water came through the open window. I still remembered the strength of his arms that gently wrapped around my back at that time, the beating of his heart clearly felt on my back, and the trembling of his passion. It was a memory I missed.

Brian, who had been hugging me without a word, released his arms and, without a word, turned his body and left the house.

"Brian! Where have you been, Brian?"

Michael, who I thought was asleep, was looking for Brian.

"Brian is gone."

I couldn't share with him the happiness I enjoyed alone with the baby, and the news that I would share face-to-face with Michael when he came. I didn't want my baby to see the drunk daddy. It was our first meeting.

'In the morning, sweetheart. Let's wait a little longer.'

I whispered as I carefully wrapped my stomach, which was not yet bulky.

"Brian, why are you here? For Anna?"

Michael said in a drunken voice as if Brian had been there. I kept my mouth shut as Michael wasn't speaking soberly.

"I know, Brian, you like Anna!"

Michael screamed as he rolled over on the bed.

I thought, 'Is this the Michael who was so sweet to me?'

Michael was a different person now.

'Brian, why are you with Anna? Anna, go to your house!'

Now Michael is like the naughty boy of his old days when he teased me when he was young, and when Brian stopped him, he would attack me even more furiously.

"Now I love Anna! Anna is my wife!"

Michael exclaimed as if Brian was still with him.

"Anna chose me!"

"Michael!"

I climbed onto the bed and hugged Michael as he struggled. It seems to me that Michael was still caught up in the emotions of his childhood. The reason he couldn't enjoy everything he had was probably because of his own inferiority complex towards Brian. After marrying, Michael was always ambitious and confident, but even after he had the baby he wanted, he still feels inferior.

"Anna, are you too? Do you like Brian?"

Michael's eyes twisted with envy.

"Don't do that, Michael."

I wrapped my arms around Michael's shoulder again. Michael's shoulders wrung violently in my arms.

"I don't know you."

"Michael!"

Finally I shouted.

"Show me! I don't know!"

Michael got up from the bed and grabbed the hem of my clothes. Michael shook the hem of my robe, and I, sitting on the bed, shook on the bed. It seemed that I could not escape from Michael's grasp.

"Michael, please!"

Michael's tone, which became more insistent the more he got drunk, seemed to be his drunken habit, and I wasn't used to that habit.

"Show me, so I can believe it!"

He shook the hem of my robe again, and I wobbled back and forth as he shook it.

"Are you ignoring me? Yeah, you've been ignoring me since I was little. You never ran into me. Don't you know that it made me feel bad? That's why you wanted to ignore me more!"

Michael was tenacious. It was as if Michael was arguing with me with clear mind.

With this thought in his heart, how he apologized to me and asked for forgiveness, all of which seemed to lie to me. How could he have been so gentle and kind to me all this time, everything seemed like hypocrisy. I didn't know what the hell Michael was really like.

“What the hell is Brian to you!”
I was out of breath. It seemed that something that had been filled up until now in my mind was pouring out. I said nothing and forgot about the baby.
“Are you ignoring me again? fuck!”
In a moment Michael's big fists flew right in front of my eyes, and I lost my balance and fell to the floor. It was as if my body had flown off a steep cliff.
"Mom!"
I fell and was lying on the floor, calling her mother and wrapping her from the stomach first. The part that I hit hard, whether it was my butt or my stomach, was very painful, but I couldn't figure out exactly which part it hurt. I couldn't even stand up and I only called my mother like a moan. As if answering, my mother's leg, which had blood dripping down before my eyes, passed. I couldn't even stand up, and like a moan, I called only my real mother, and at that moment, as if answering, my mother's legs, which were bleeding, passed in front of my eyes. It was the leg of a mother who died while giving birth. Then, the two red lines in the diagnostic machine seemed to run down the two legs that I didn't know if it was my mother's or mine.
"No!"
I screamed and shook my head violently. The memory of the blood flowing down my mother's legs should not come to mind at this point. I shook my head and tried to force myself to stand up. I couldn't stand up as my body was stuck on the floor.

When I woke up, I was in an unfamiliar place. My mother and Sua were there and Michael was crying.
“Anna!”
My mother's eyes were red. Sua was supporting her mother-in-law, letting her tears flow, and Michael was standing by the bed, crying continuously, with an exhausted look that didn't even have time to stroke his messy hair.
"Mother!"
I wanted to ask, 'Why is everyone crying?' But I couldn't. It was because I was afraid.
“Why didn’t you tell me, Anna!”
Said Michael crying. I thought it must be baby news.
“I was going to do it in the morning.”

The scene from last night passed. Last night, he drank with me after Brian left. He doubted Brian and didn't believe me, I thought it was a long-standing feeling of inferiority.

"I didn't know. I didn't know my baby."

Did Michael really know our baby? I hadn't even shown my baby to him yet.

"I also knew it during the day. I was waiting to make you happy."

"Anna!"

Michael collapsed on the bed I was lying on. It was a cry that I had never heard before. I could guess from his cry what had happened.

"Michael!"

I grabbed Michael's shoulder with one hand and shook it. Michael's massive body shook violently in my grasp. It was as if I was shaking in Michael's hand on the bed.

"Why are you crying, Michael?"

But Michael didn't say it was okay. My mother and Sua also cried.

"Anna!"

Eventually, my mother called, and the ominous memory of the red blood running down my Peruvian mother's legs came to mind.

"Why are you doing this to me, Mom!"

Suddenly I shouted, as if it was my real mother's fault. It was Quechua.

"Anna!"

Michael hugged me as I struggled.

"No, no!"

As I struggled in Michael's arms, I lost consciousness. It was chaos.

20. To be Punished

I came home. It was my room in my mother's house, where I could see Lake Ontario outside the window in the winter when I couldn't go up to the treehouse and play the zamponya.
The words I had to vomit were fulI, but I kept them inside. My family members, who had no idea what had happened, lingered around me, feeling very frustrated. Only Brian, who couldn't possibly tell parents about Michael's drinking, seemed to blame himself for leaving me alone that night.

'It's not your fault, Brian.'

I wanted to say that, but I didn't even want to say it out loud. Nothing would change if I said anything. Living was so ridiculous and boring that I wanted to disappear without a sound.

Was this how your mother felt when she lost her way home? My mother said the road disappeared on the way. How absurd was her? Life that came like a dream, my baby also suddenly went away with half a day of joy, so I am absurd. It's so ridiculous. My path has disappeared like my mother's path.

Strictly speaking, it wasn't just Michael's fault. It was my fault for not noticing the immature life that had already came to me as my baby a few weeks ago. So, I was not worthy to be a mother. I was more ashamed than my mother who enjoyed the short spring sunshine, didn't even know that young Brian had been abducted. But I was still upset. It seemed like I couldn't live like this.

Laying down, I silently quarreled with anyone that came to my mind. I argued with my Peruvian mother, who is not in this world, asking, 'You must have been beautiful at times, but why did you always appear to me in the form of blood?'

I argued with Brian, saying, 'why did you make me come to this land by calling me 'Anna' when I was a mamani'. I quarreled with Michael. I got angry and asked why you couldn't leave me in my bad memories so that I hated you for the rest of my life, and why, why, why, why did you call me to meet me in the first place? In the end, I even started arguing with my baby who didn't exist in this world now.

'You can't come and leave like that, baby!'

And then I scratched and abused myself. I really wanted to disappear too, without a trace.

My mother, who was depressed, went into the kitchen, made food, and brought hot food into my room.

But I didn't eat, I didn't talk, I didn't leave the room. Even when Michael came in the morning and evening saying he would go and see my face, I didn't meet him, and when Michael's parents came, I didn't say anything.

"I think we'll have to wait a little while for Anna to settle down, Joan."

My mother-in-law wondered why I didn't tell anyone in the family when I was pregnant, and my mother, who didn't know about it, must have been even more upset.

"I didn't know Michael was still drinking," my mother said.

As it all started because of Michael's drinking, my mother, who thought Michael was not involved in alcohol, brought it up. My mother and father, who believed Michael had already stopped drinking, were outraged that what he said was a lie.

My parents never heard from me or from Brian that Michael started drinking again. I wondered if my parents could have guessed through the words that Michael mumbled while crying at the hospital bedside. My parents probably also speculated that the miscarriage had something to do with Michael's drinking. But because I kept my mouth shut, my parents didn't know for sure. My mother will still think I'm lucky to have Sua, who is like a friend to me.

I was looking at the lake. The Sea Doo, wanting to enjoy the late summer, roared and spewed white foam. Thinking about Michael's words that it's called a motorcycle in the water, I was thinking of Michael again.

Michael preferred speedboats, also called cigar boats, rather than sailboats moving slowly in the wind.

'I'm dizzy, go slow!'
When I first got into Michael's boat, I closed my eyes tightly because I feared the boat would overturn. As I was sprinting at high speed with my eyes closed, the motion sickness got worse.
'Anna, you have to get motion sick a few times! Then you can enjoy it!'
Even though we were right next to each other, because of the roar, we had to speak out loud to each other.
Meanwhile, I gradually became Michael and I was enjoying speed. Michael and I would float a boat on the Niagara River in front of our house and back to Lake Erie against the rushing water between the piers of the American railroad and the piers of the Peace Bridge.
Looking down from my mother's tree house, Ontario becomes Peru's Lake Titicaca to me, but I couldn't feel Lake Titicaca when I cut the water with a speedboat.
There was a reed forest on Lake Titicaca I remembered, and there were flocks of birds, deep blue skies, sunlight, fishing boats, and extremely simple lives of people with tanned skin. But, when the speedboat roared, the water turned over, and foamy motion sickness took my place, I couldn't recall the scene of that humble life. There was only thrill and pleasure.
'It was a kind of show, that I wasn't weak. As I parted the current and the air, I got a feeling of wanting to blow away all my chronic weaknesses.'
That was why Michael started his first boat ride.
Like Michael, I felt the pleasure of speed. I gradually got used to the noise and speed rather than the silence, and I was becoming a Michael who enjoyed thrills.

"Can I come in, Anna?"
I looked at the messy water surface the boat had passed and thought of Michael, when Sua knocked. I opened the door and stepped out of the way, and Sua, who was holding a coffee tray on a tray, cautiously stepped in.
"I want to drink coffee together."
With coffee, Sua was talking to me.
The image of Sua when she first came from Korea flashed through my mind. Her eyes were as deep as a well, and she was a calm woman who only smiled when she answered 'yes' or 'no' to her parents-in-law's

questions.
Now that she was a mother of two, Sua couldn't be quiet anymore. There was a time when Sua told me that she was busy chasing baby Ian, who was running and looking forward only. From that moment on, I thought, 'She couldn't be quiet any longer because Sua had to talk to Ian at Ian's eye level, and she had to tell me the story of how Ian was growing up.' Moreover, she was now a mother of two.

"Thank you, Sua."

I said as I took my cup of coffee.

But she only fiddled with her cup of coffee, as if she didn't know what to say. I also kept my mouth shut. A fog seemed to have subsided between them.

"I don't know what to say, Anna."

Sua opened her mouth first. Sua had a cheek that looked like crying would come out.

I put the coffee cup on the table. Then I took Sua's hand. After she found out that it was me that Brian had loved, and after the day she said 'I'm sorry', it was the first time I held Sua's hand.

"You don't have to say anything, Sua."

"But, it still doesn't make sense, it's too harsh."

Suddenly, Sua uttered her words violently as if she were arguing with me. So, she was complaining about why I endured all this nonsense and why I was so calm. Sua's unfamiliar appearance, wiping the dripping tears with her palm, looked fierce in my eyes. It must have come from the heart of a mother of her two children.

Sua's words were clearly resentful, but in my heart there was no resentment at all. Rather, a lump that was trapped inside me, inflating its body like a rubber balloon, seemed to provoke me. It was a lump of crying that I had been holding back inside me.

Instead of answering, I hugged my stomach. It was chaff that did not save a life. My stomach should have swelled up little by little every day, so that I could enjoy the joy of full term, but instead of the sound of breathing, it was filled with sadness, anger, and unjust screams.

"It's been a while, but you were a mother too, a mother lost her child,"
Sua spoke up again as if she couldn't understand me, who ignored the harsh facts and insisted on silence.

Sua's words meant that a mother who lost a child has no reason to be conscious of other things, so why can't you cry as you wanted.

At that moment, one word of Sua's resentments, "You lost your child' became an ember that dug into my heart and ignited a fire in the core of me. In an instant, a fire broke out, and it transferred to my anger and spread to my sadness. And it began to set and burn.
My stomach became a fire in an instant.
The heat soared. I hugged my shriveled chest and twisted my body.
"Mom!"
A moan broke out in Quechua. The tears I had been holding on began to burst and flow down. Then hot tears ran down my cheeks and wet neck. Tears were unbearable for my eyes. Sua hugged me and cried.

It seemed that Michael came again in the evening.
Michael would have noticed my parents' moods and my parents and Brian would not have welcomed Michael.
Even though I kept my mouth shut, everyone in my family was guessing that there must have been a big trouble between me and Michael. The hard-earned life was aborted, and instead of going back to Michael's house, I came to my parents' house and remained silent until now. Brian and parents, who knew nothing of what happened in between, were imagining all sorts of things and would not be able to welcome Michael. Above all, it was because I turned away from Michael.

"I need to see Anna, Mother."
Michael was pleading with my mother, saying that he must meet me today, who had already refused to see him even after several days of morning and evening visits.
"What the hell happened, Michael? Tell us."
Mother's voice came from downstairs. But Michael kept silent.
"I'm going to see Anna, Mother."
Then I heard Michael's footsteps walking up the stairs. Being stubborn, my mother might not have resisted or deliberately allowed it.
"Anna."
Michael stood in front of the closed door and called me. I didn't answer.
"I have to see you today. I will not go without meeting you."
There was so much to say and I thought I would go crazy if I didn't pour it all out, but I didn't want to say anything.
When there was no response, Michael, who seemed to be standing still

for a moment, turned the doorknob. He was ready to come in even if he broke the door. I didn't lock the door.

"Anna!"

Michael tried to open it with all his might, but when it opened too easily, Michael was surprised and hesitated, unable to enter the room willingly. Michael entered the room.

"Why is your face like this?"

Michael's voice was already weeping. Michael's face was just as bad as mine. If our faces were normal at this point, something would have been wrong.

"Oh, Anna!"

Michael hugged me.

"I saw it! The two red lines you were about to show me ...Oh, God!"

Michael flopped down on the spot and covered his face with both hands. It was as if I had sat down on the spot with both hands covering my face at Michael's teasing a long time ago.

So, Michael's words meant the diagnostic machine that announced the baby's existence with the two bright red lines that day. Rejoicing with the tester in hand, I thought of calling Michael. However, I had put it on the table, thinking that I would give him the diagnostic kit as a gift when Michael came. And I forgot about it after something horrible happened.

I wanted to shout, "What was the difference when you saw the life that left, leaving just two short red lines?"

"How am I?"

'I don't know, neither do I. I'm lost too!'

I shouted to Michael inside.

"I remembered how you waited for me that day and what I did while watching it."

Michael knelt down in front of me, wrapping his face again with his hands.

'Do you remember everything?'

It was clear that the baby, who had shown me his presence with the two red lines, had pulled up the memories of his father, who was drunk instead of me.

"Stop it, Michael. What's the use of saying that now?"

But I was cool. I also had a lot to say, but now I don't want to. He said he had already remembered everything, so he said he knew all his mistakes. What more should I say? It was the same with me that I couldn't be proud of myself in front of that life.

"I did something bad to you. And to our baby who came to us hard..."

Michael twisted his back.

Father's tears of lamentation were natural, so I did not comfort Michael even if he cried.

"What should I do, Anna?"

Michael looked up at me with her face covered in tears.

"Go back, Michael! Never come again!"

I turned away. I had to be harsh in front of Michael's tears.

"Don't do that, Anna!"

'Drink again, become addicted again, and become a nuisance, whatever you want!'

I couldn't even say those words out loud.

Michael's hands grabbed my feet. Tears dripped down my feet.

Can weep be forgiven of all our sins? Can I be forgiven too?

He and I were people who had nothing to say to the life of the red stripe. Both of them were greedy but not prepared.

I bent my knees and got Michael up. Michael got up and looked at me.

I wiped his face with the skirt. He was a person who rebelled and wandered because he could not enjoy everything he had, became addicted at a young age, and eventually lost his child.

He was a person who would suffer himself even if I didn't bother him.

He was the one who would carry that burden for the rest of his life.

"We should be punished."

I said looking into Michael's eyes. Michael looked at me with childish eyes. And nodded his head.

"I will take that punishment. Don't say don't come, Anna."

Michael begged.

"That's the punishment, to get away from each other and rethink this relationship."

"Anna, what are you thinking?"

Michael grabbed my shoulder and shook me.

"I will. I'll think again. You should too, Michael."

After thinking apart like that, if it was our conclusion that the two of us would meet again, then I would go back to my house, and if neither of us thought it was the case, then we would just part.

"If we go back to the past without this kind of punishment, wouldn't it be too much of a shame?”

I was already stubborn. We were apart from each other Separated from each other and should soberly consider our relationship.
Michael's eyes looked like they were terrified. He might recall that hour of therapy. That will be a punishment for him, Michael. He will be punished more for the mistake of bringing back the past that he did not want to go through again, and the mistake of disappointing me for believing the word ‘I got it’.

“This will be our last chance to think about our relationship.”
I couldn't be kind to the end.

21. I miss Peru

After I was released from the hospital, I was still staying at my mother's house.
I don't know if I'll ever go back to our house where Michael is. We don't know how long, but we should stay apart and think seriously about each other and our future. It is the punishment we inflicted on us.

'Let's rest a lot when we get home, Anna.'
When I had to go home from the hospital that day, Michael was ready to take me home. It was natural, regardless of the reason for the miscarriage and how I felt about it.
'I'll take Anna, Michael.'
But my mother, who came with Sua, ignored Michael's words and said that she would take me to my parents' house. It was unexpected for me as well, so I was in a bit of a mess between my mother and Michael.
'Anna will go home with me and rest. When Anna says she wants to go home, I'll let her go.'
'Mother!'
My mother's resolute words with thorns left me bewildered, and Michael looked at my mother as if it were nonsense. Michael had a look on his face, asking why Anna's house was her mother's house. Even to my ears, my mother's words sounded to mean that she couldn't let me go because she couldn't trust him. Michael, who seemed to be taking me home, stiffened for a moment. It seemed that my mother's words discouraged Michael's spirit
'Let's go home.'
'To the house I...'
Michael, who was pressed by my mother's spirit, said that he would

take me to my mother's house, telling me to rest for a few days but, then, he eventually had to finally gave up even that in front of my mother who cut him off, saying, 'Don't worry, Michael'.

It was the first time for me to see my mother so cold and so determined. I knew it was normal to go home with Michael, but I couldn't say a word and had no choice but to get into Sua's car.

"Sometimes you need words that you don't mean, Anna."

This was what my mother said in the car on the way home. It meant that my mother was intentionally cold-hearted towards Michael.

'Your home is where your mother is. I'm never going to let you go if you don't want it.'

My mother was still stubborn.

That's how I started spending most of my time at my mother's house with her.

My mother enjoyed gardening, cooking, sewing, and cooking. There was not a single thing in the house that my mother had not touched, and my mother, who used to sing to me while teaching me how to organize the house, was slowly losing her memory, and gradually forgetting to smile like a little child. When my mother, who used to brighten up the atmosphere in the house, reduced the number of words, the family members also lowered their voices.

My father, who had lost energy more than anyone else, was losing more motivation than my mother. He was like a child who had lost his mother. Looking back, the bright energy in the house came from my mother's bright voice, and my father must have known that the bright energy would always fill the house like air. But my mother was not silent about what I had been through.

Once I had regained some of my energy, my mother remembered everything I thought she had now forgotten.

She said, "Your mom was so careless again."

My mother regretted herself for making me choose Michael as if I was throwing myself away because she had separated me from Brian, and she blamed herself for saying that it was her own fault that she thought I would have a good life with Michael.

"What the hell have I done to my children's lives?"

My mother regretted herself as she hit her chest with her one hand.

My mother, who was slowly losing her memory after losing her way, scratched herself, remembering so clearly what she could have forgotten.

At my mother's house, I often thought of Michael. I was also worried that Michael would exhaust himself by drinking again and so he would get another treatment. It was what Michael feared the most.
My thoughts on Michael started with worrying about him more than resentment and ended with worrying. Even though I knew the result so clearly, I was sober.
Even though I thought and worried about Michael several times a day, but I never called or contacted him.
It was a promise in the first place, a punishment that was inflicted on us, and it was taken for granted.
My parents spent a lot of time with me, but they didn't ask about Michael. It must have been because of the thought that the parents were disrespectful to the son-in-law who made his daughter like this, and it was probably because of the thought that mentioning Michael would only make me sick.

As the weather turned cold, I stopped on my way to the tree house and played with my mother, and occasionally played the zamponya. It was the musical instrument that I put down from my hands while I was with Michael.
“I want to hear El Condor Pasa, Anna.”
Today, my mother remembered the name of the song correctly, so I was happy to get the zamponya. My mother, who knew the meaning of my expression, said, 'How can I forget, it's a song my daughter plays.'
I put the zamponya on my lower lip as if it was about to touch my lower lip, and then breathed in as if spitting out my upper lip with my tongue.

-O Almighty Condor, Master of Heaven,
take us home in the Andes
I want to go back to
where I lived with my Inca compatriots
that is my earnest wish
Almighty Condor, wait for me in the Inca square of Cusco.
Let us walk through Machu Picchu and Huayna Picchu-

‘You have to make a sound by exhaling the air on the tip of your

tongue.'
When my brother Mario blew the zamponya, he would mutter to himself while I was watching him. 'As if spitting out, and as if the sound of the remaining breath blowing away, as if the rustling of reeds swaying in the wind, and as if it was the sound of longing for the exhaled breath that had already disappeared and could not be caught.'
My brother put air on the tip of his tongue and made a melody as if playing with it, but I couldn't understand why the melody was always sad in my ears.
Why did Mario kill people?
Why did my brother die in prison?
The life of my sad brother, who died while playing only sad songs, was left intact in the zamponya, so I was sad every time I played the zamponya.
The musical instrument made by my father by tying a reed tube with a five-colored string woven by my mother, a samponya that soaks in the marks of my mother and father, and even the sound of my brother's breathing, followed me as far away as Canada.
When my father put the zampoyna in my bag that my brother gave me while he was in prison, said, 'Don't forget, you are a daughter of Peru.'

When I was playing El Condor Pasa with the zamponya, I missed the place where there was Lake Titicaca, the water birds flew, the traces of my mother, and my father and brother. I was born in Peru and raised until the age of seven, but I had never been to Machu Picchu, the Inca Hanging Garden, the Lost City of the Sun, because I had never left the town. My Peruvian father said that one of the paintings in the Natsuka Desert was clearly a condor. Ah, the Nazca desert with mysterious geometric shapes, various ruins, and my hometown in Peru was the substance of my longing to visit someday.

"Anna, why do tears well up in my eyes when you play?"
My mother said while I was playing El Condor Pasa, thinking that Lake Ontario far out the window was Lake Titicaca. Mother was crying. As she lost her memory, my mother stopped talking and often wept.

"Why couldn't I have thought that even you, when you were young, needed your brother, your father, and your hometown? I also went through the pain of losing a child, and I couldn't understand the feelings of your father and brother who had to let you go."

It seemed that the zamponya melody evoked a very old memory of my mother. After Brian as a child went through the dread of kidnapping, my mother was only obsessed with the idea of needing someone to be with Brian, she said.
My mother took my hand.

"You are such a blessing to me. But I'm sorry, Anna. I've never regretted raising you as my daughter, but now that I'm older I sometimes think that it's my selfishness."

"Mother!"

I took my mother's wrinkled, limp hands. I hated seeing my mother hurt because of me.

"Anna, shall we go to Peru?"

My mother looked up at me with her eyes twinkling. My mother knew the true nature of the longing within me.

"Yes, mother, we go to Cusco and to Lake Titicaca."

It was Cusco, the capital of the Inca, where the descendants of the old Inca desperately wanted to meet the new immortal condor, and Lake Titicaca, the home of mother, father, and brother that I could not forget even in my dreams.

"Okay, let's go, with me."

Mother nodded her head.

From then on, my mother and I began to have the same dream, to go to my hometown together, to the place where my mother and I first met. Titicaca, the highest sky lake in South America, created by the melt water of the Andean mountains, is the lake believed to have originated from the Inca civilization. It was a poor life, but the spirit of the Inca was higher and deeper than the sky lake. Somewhere beyond the horizon of Lake Titicaca where the golden sunset spreads, there must be Cusco and Machu Picchu. Peru is where people who embrace the spirit of the immortal bird condor live. The land where the memory is now hazy, the place where my father caught turcha and the sound of the zamponya my brother was playing with his eyes closed, passed through my head, calling for nostalgia again. It was a hometown I hadn't been to since I left.

22. Misunderstanding

When I saw people on the farm, it was the beginning of spring, and when they left, it was autumn.

In the early spring, workers from Jamaica and Mexico roamed the plantations, figuring out what to do in due season, some of whom were experts, already working in one field for many years.

After Diego left, even though my mother had long left the housework to someone else, she nevertheless always took care of the flowers as well as when she was healthy. It was for the health of her body and mind, and it was also what my mother did best. This year too, the garden that my mother and I took care of was full of flowers until late autumn, but now it withers and is preparing for winter.

I was already used to taking care of flowers, so while I was living with Michael for nine years, I turned my house into a flower garden. I was taking care of spring flowers this year as well, but I suddenly came to my mother's house in midsummer, so I was curious about the flowers, but I didn't call.

I didn't care if the flowers in my house were blooming or withering because Michael and I suggested we get away from each other and think deeply about our relationship. Just because my mother needed exercise, and because my mother, who had many troubles that often happened to her, had to bury her thoughts, I often took care of flowers in the garden with my mother.

Having spent a lot of time with my mother, I thought that I would like to do everything for my mother as she did for me when I was a child. It was that I became her companion, her daughter, and her friend. Mother gradually became more dependent on me, and I was willing to become her will, and it was like being reborn as a daughter.

I was able to say the word 'no', which I was not used to, while spending a lot of time with my mother. When I said 'no' instead of 'yes' at the moment when I should have said 'no', I felt like I was finally becoming my mother's real daughter.

'Call Michael one more time, Anna.'

This was what my mother said one day while caring for flowers in the garden.

In fact, even if it wasn't my mother's words, I was curious about him and missed him. How he eats, how he sleeps with wine every day in a house without me, and what his house looks like after a long absence, above all else, I wanted to see Michael.

But since it was an appointment, I never went to my house, which is less than an hour from my mother's house, and I never called.

We were separated and sometimes bitterly resenting each other, desperately missing more time, paying the price of sacrifice for letting go of the life of our baby who had come to us with difficulty after nine years. It was a time to atone for the life that had to pass without any fault. But my mother told me to call Michael.

'No!'

My mother was unfamiliar with my answer, as I had never once said 'no' to my mother's request, but I felt like I was getting closer to my mother.

As I was giving the answers I wanted to, I felt that I was breaking down the 'carefulness' that was between my mother and me, or that I was the only one feeling.

My answer, 'no', meant the same thing as Brian grumbled at his mother. It was something I wanted to do too.

At the same time, autumn passed and the workers who had finished harvesting the grapes left for their country with the promise of next year.

Now it was a deep winter.

Instead of spending time in the tree house and garden, I borrowed books from the local library for my mother and I to read.

Along with my mother's favorite romance novels, I borrowed novels and books about interiors, gardens, and cooking.

Canada's long and deep winter is a season that can make people's hearts depressed, but with the cheerful sounds of Brian's two children, my zamponya melody, books, and playing with my mother, I don't get bored of the long winter.

It snowed several times to cover people's ankles, but Canadians already knew, especially driving in the snow. And when it snows, the first thing to do is to remove the snow from the road with a snow plow, so there is no big problem. I went to the library with my mother, but today my mother was taking an afternoon nap, so I went out alone. I was about to return the book I had read and borrow something to read again.

Every time I looked at the books listed in the library, I thought of Diego. The novel that Diego would have finished was also on the library shelf someday, waiting for me to borrow it. The scene of Diego driving a lawnmower and writing a novel in front of the computer still doesn't come naturally to me as an act of a single person, but the two different images were attractive to me. Diego, who used his body and mind to his heart's content, was a man who lived a wonderful life.

My face blushes involuntarily at the thought that the scene of my parting with Brian, which happened that night while I was picking up frozen grapes, might be in Diego's novel. It was the harvest season again, and I felt lonely thinking that it would never happen again.

Those desperate, precious, and sad times have passed and I am in a new time. It was time with Michael. What will Michael and I conclude between the two of us through this long period of silence? As it was a bad relationship from the first meeting, I didn't know whether the nine years would end in a bad relationship, or if I would trust more and build a relationship that would never waver again. However, what I felt while living away from Michael was that along with hatred, I still miss him deeply. I didn't know if this concentration of longing would cover up the hatred, or how much greater resentment and frustration Michael would create.

As the parking lot door went up, the cold air from outside was brought in. It was a gust of wind that blew through Lake Ontario. The snow that had already fallen a few times did not melt as the wind got stronger and became a white carpet along the furrows of the vineyard. Bare vines seemed to dance while stretching their arms toward the sky with their claws. Group dance on the white carpet. A winter tree with its leaves removed was sensual to my eyes, like the back of a naked woman.

I was about to get into the car with my scarf wrapped around, then,

I saw a car coming into the house from the winery. There was no one visiting my mother's house at this time, and I noticed that it was a familiar car. I still couldn't recognize the driver, so I stood there, staring intently at the car coming home.
It was Michael's car.
Suddenly my heart started pounding and I gently pressed it with one hand. I thought Michael had been patient for a long time, but has he finally made up his mind about our relationship? Other than that, there was no reason to come to see me. I got out of the parking lot and waited for Michael.
Michael shouted as he got out of the car. Michael had a beard and it reminded me of the day we first met when Michael called before we got married.
"Anna!"
"Michael?"
I said, trying to subdue the urge to run and snuggle into his arms. Come to think of it, he was still my husband, whom I could rest in his arms.
Perhaps because he drank a lot, he seemed a bit skinny. I didn't know if he was actually drunk or not. Neither Michael nor I purposely contacted each other, and Brian didn't say anything, so we didn't know each other's well-being.
"Oh, Anna, how are you?"
Michael, who seemed to be approaching, hugging me, hesitated and stopped in front of me to say hello. It was as if there was a line in front of him and me that he couldn't cross.
"Can I hug you?"
And he politely asked for my permission.
'The reason for being so polite...'
Before answering, I was thinking. It would mean that Michael had already made up his mind.
"Yes."
I answered briefly with a stern expression on my face. Whatever the conclusion, it was something I had to face anyway. I wanted to be more calm. Michael, who had been faltering a step away, came over and looked into my face first. Then he covered my face with his hands and pulled me by the shoulders and held him in his arms, standing still.
Michael seemed to have changed a lot, with the prudence that had

filtered out all recklessness and politeness that made me feel distant. Michael, who was holding me silently, released me from his arms and looked at me again.

"Aren't you in pain?"

His words and expressions were restrained.

"No, are you?"

Like Michael, I had no choice but to reduce the number of words.

"It was hard, everything."

Instead of saying 'I was doing well,' Michael said, 'it was hard'. It seemed to mean that he had a difficult decision.

"I'm on my way to the library, will you take me?"

I was hoping he would take me out somewhere other than in the library.

"Okay, let's go."

I got into Michael's car and Michael followed the parkway, not the library. It was the way home.

During the 40-minute drive from my mother's house to Michael's, we didn't say much. I have so much to say that I don't know what I should say first, but Michael cut down his words, so I couldn't express my words by myself. In the end, our relationship seemed to come to an end without being able to say all the words inside.

It was a time of calmly accepting any conclusion, but it was bittersweet than I expected. Why was this conclusion unexpected? I wanted to cry.

This sudden feeling of wanting to cry was also completely unexpected.

What the hell did I expect, while hating so much? Why did it flow into my life when it will all flow away in the end?

Michael stopped the car in front of the house while I promised myself that I must take care of my heart right now and never show any tears.

My house, without a hostess, was crouching on the spot, more eerie than winter.

"Let's go in, it's cold."

Michael opened the front door and let me in first. As I entered my house, I felt like a guest.

It may be a house that will never come again even as a guest. The house where I lived for nine years, the house that I touched every nook and cranny. A house with my favorite kitchen items. A house where I have changed the bedding, my underwear, my pajamas, and even my outerwear. A house that stays in its own place without an owner even when the seasons change.

Maybe Michael had already cleaned out all of my belongings. The things of a woman whose heart is gone. What kind of love remains in those things, so Michael is still keeping my things? No matter how much I thought about it, it didn't seem possible. Thinking like that, my regrets seemed to go away.

Yes, this is not the time for that, but if he asks his wife, who came home after summer and autumn, 'Shall we have a glass of wine?' oh, no, no, but if he pretends to take off even the thick scarf around my neck, my heart, filled with twists and turns, seemed like it would be relieved soon enough, but Michael was now showing the behavior of welcoming guests who were about to leave.

But who knows, if Michael comes out with a glass of wine, I'll get drunk while just holding the empty glass he hands me, or if he puts his hand on the scarf around my neck, I'll hold his hand to me. And who knows what other impulses will arise next?

Even if we were separated from each other for some inevitable reason and had time to reconsider our relationship, if the slightest occasion, such as holding an empty glass or holding his hand that would touch my neck, happened, it would be a link to restore our relationship again. We were still a couple.

But from the beginning until now, he was showing me politeness that I was not used to, and the politeness that made me feel the proper distance because it was too heavy. The more he does, the more my feelings seem to be twisted, and I feel uncomfortable even in my house.

'He must have really stopped drinking,'

I was thinking to myself, looking at his back as he turned around before the sink and prepared for the tea.

Thinking it was cold in the house, Michael turned on the fireplace switch and a blue gas flame flew through the imitation firewood.

The house that caught my eye was far more neat and tidy than I had expected. The kitchen sink area was clean and the floors looked like they had been vacuumed. It was as if someone was running a house.

'I was worried for nothing.'

Laughter leaked out from within.

"Let's have tea."
Michael brought two cups of tea I didn't even know the name of and placed them in front of me. The teacup was familiar to my eyes. It was the teacup my mother bought me.
'What did I come here with Michael to check?'
I had no desire to raise my cup and drink tea. I wanted to get out of this house.
"How does it feel to be home after a long time?"
said Michael, holding up his teacup. Instead of answering, I just smiled.
Michael might have guessed that I wanted to get out of this house quickly. Maybe he had brought me for that purpose.
"I can live this well without you,"
Come to think of it, it was Michael, a young Michael who tormented his opponents and looked around with more excitement and laughter.
'I can't believe I followed him all the way here. How much more do I want to be teased...?'
Without knowing it, I was hoping that he would take me somewhere. Just thinking about it really made me laugh.
"Michael, what brought you to my mother's house?"
However, I couldn't get up from my seat right away, so I asked while holding a teacup.
Now, even though there was no reason to know it, I couldn't find anything else to say other than this one. I've already checked everything, but why did I ask Michael this question? Because I wanted to get more shock from Michael? Anyway, it spilled water.
"I really forgot. I have something to give you."
Then Michael got up and pulled an envelope out of the pocket of his coat. He held the envelope in front of me.
'Yeah, that was it!'
I felt like I was falling to the distant floor.
My feelings at this moment were the same as the feeling that I felt when I fell from the bed while instinctively avoiding Michael's fist. It was my body then, but it is my heart now. It seemed as though I would never be able to get up and live completely again if my body and mind had been torn apart like this.
I put the envelope I received on the table. Nine years of time with Michael went by at the speed of light. It was time to cover all my

nightmares of childhood. If it wasn't for me, no, it wasn't for the lives we lost, at least I wouldn't be in this desperate mood. Life is gone, Michael is gone, and I am the only one left.
Life is gone, Michael is gone, and I am the only one left.
But no regrets. Living with my parents who brought me in, I have already learned that what I can do is 'adapt' to things that are beyond my ability. Just as we had no choice but to let go of our lost live even from our hearts, we just have to pass our nine years in the same way. Even if it flows, traces will remain, but what can I do? It is also a part of my life that I should embrace.

At that point, I thought I should get up. But Michael brought me here, so I needed Michael's help on the way back to my mother's house.
I got up with the envelope on the table, 'Can you take me?
"Are you going already?"
"Already..?"
No matter how much I asked, 'Can you take me?', his answer should be, 'Don't go'
Am I not the wife who came home after a long time? So, his words seemed to mean to live longer like this in our respective places. Now that I have the documents in the envelope, it means that our relationship will end soon.
"I will read this when I get home and answer it."
I went to the front door thinking it wasn't worth looking at anymore.
"I want to hear what you think, when will I hear it?"
Michael was impatient.
"Don't worry, it won't take long."
I didn't want to hold on to it foolishly, because it's something I've been thinking about countless times. I was just afraid because I had to go through another loss. If I lose them one by one, what will be left of me last? Thinking about it, I want to let go of everything before I lose everything, but I couldn't do anything about the fear that came over me.
On the way home, neither Michael nor I talked much.
I wanted to cry again.
I didn't even want to go even to my mother's house, but this winter, I had no place to go and no one I wanted to meet.

"Did you borrow a book from the library, Anna?"

Waking up from my nap, my mother seemed to be waiting for a book. I hesitated for a moment, whether or not I should tell my mother that I met Michael and have been to our house. But with no book in my hand, I was forced to talk about meeting Michael.

"Actually, I met Michael, Mother."

I decided to tell you the truth. It wasn't something to be hidden anyway.

"Michael?"

Even my mother was surprised. My mother would already know, that there was a serious problem between me and Michael. She didn't ask if she would offend me, but she would have been watching.

"I was going to the library, but he came so I asked for a ride. He took me home."

But how could I tell my mother about what I saw and felt and the envelope I brought with me? I really hate that my mother was shocked and hurt because of me.

"Yeah, what did Michael say? Didn't he tell you to come?"

My mother asked a very motherly question. How would he respond if it wasn't me but Brian?

'You don't know Michael that much?'

Brian might be arguing with mother.

Now that I felt that the distance between me and my mother was gone, I wanted to confront my mother like that, but I couldn't. Actually, it was because my mother spoke very motherly words. What mother would want to see her daughter live in her mother's home away from her husband for a long time?

Having nothing to say, I looked at my mother for a moment. What would my mother say if I answered, 'I think Michael made up his mind, I just got an envelope with our divorce papers in it'?

Unable to express what I had to say, I couldn't handle the things that had been trapped inside me suddenly came up all at once. I could still suppress something that stings my throat, but I couldn't help the tears that had already reached my eyes and were welling up.

"What's going on, Anna!"

"Mother!"

Without realizing it, I fell on my mother's lap. I really wanted to cry anyway.

"What happened, Anna! What did Michael say?"

I wanted to tell my mother every single detail. From that moment of my baby's day until now, I was filled with things that I couldn't resist and pressed inside.

"You mean Michael made my daughter cry again? He is such a bad guy..."

My mother stopped brushing my hair and patting my back. It was clear that my mother was also angry. As my mother was even more angry than me, so in the end I couldn't say anything. However, at least in my heart I wanted to shield Michael from his mother's wrath.

23. Reversal

After a short winter break, Brian's two children had to go to school. I left the house together to take the two children to the Bus Shelter.
For children, cold weather was just a characteristic of winter. Even when the white snow covered their calves, the children laughed and ran forward and backward. I took two children's bags and walked slowly behind them.
Canadian parents seemed to be relatively bold in raising their children. Parents did not overdress their children even in the long, cold winters. School started right after two-week Halloween holidays, which included Christmas and New Year holidays, and it was a deep winter, so it snowed almost every day and the weather was terrible. But the children went to school in the cold and enjoyed skating, skiing and hockey. All were winter sports. For children in a country with long and snowy winters, winter was just a season to enjoy. They were strong and healthy children who were not afraid of the cold.

There were times when I felt empty as if I had nowhere to put my mind. The emptiness was due to not having such coveted children in my arms.
If I thought that there would never be another chance for me to conceive in my life, I felt as if I had lost one of my most precious hopes. I wanted to ask someone why are you doing this to me. Until now, my real mother was that someone. She was a mother who died while giving birth. When I think of her, she was such a pitiful woman who had to close her eyes leaving her young children and her husband behind. Nevertheless, the reason I chose my real mother as the object I could freely complain about may be that my deceased mother was

the most sympathetic to me, or that I could not have another object as comfortable as my mother to expose my grievances.

"Aunt Anna and my dad went to school this way, didn't you"

Brian's daughter, Rachel, looked back at me and asked while playing with her brother Ian. Maybe Brian told Rachel about it.

Yes, this was the way I used to play with Brian while laughing and singing. It was the road I walked with Brian on my back. And this was the road that Brian insisted on carrying me on his back when the two of us were teenagers.

It was the road where Brian insisted that if I didn't put him on his back, he would carry me with him. How can I tell my life without this road?

"Yeah, your dad and aunt were playing around just like you."

I couldn't believe I didn't have such a coveted child! A feeling of frustration that I could never overcome seemed to block my eyes.

For something beyond my ability, I was able to cope with it as a method of adaptation from an early age, but this was difficult. I could raise my baby well, and I thought I could be a good mother too, but I fell down several times a day in front of this harsh reality as I won't even have a chance to have a lovely baby.

The three of us, arriving at the Bus-Stop Shelter a little early, went inside. It was a small house my father built for Brian and me to wait for the bus when it was cold, when it was hot, when it was raining.

'This is the house where my grandson will wait for the bus.'

A long time ago, when Brian and I were college students, and when Brian told father that we didn't need a shelter at the bus stop anymore, that's what father told us.

Even though Brian and I were no longer at the bus stop, father would check the damaged part of the bus stop shelter every year for the grandchildren.

At that time, I had a secret dream, that it would be nice if Brian and my child would wait for the bus at this bus stop house. Now that I think about it, it was a really unpredictable thought.

The tree house that my father had built was still being used as a playground for the two children, but now, instead of my mother, Sua climbed up and down the ladder with cookies and drinks.

Every winter, when the fishy smell of water starts to rise from Lake Ontario, my father checks first the tree house and the ladder hanging over the oak tree before Brian and I climb up.

Brian, who said that there was no more waiting for the bus, and asked to remove the stop, did not say that the mystery house should be removed. Rather, he does not neglect the task of checking whether the tree house is still strong after taking the place of his father. Perhaps it was because he thought that the tree house would leave a special memory for the children just as the memories of the tree house were precious to Brian.

Just like my mother did in the past, Sua made a pretty cushion and put it in the tree house. In addition, Sua showed her sense and hung the children's favorite pictures on the wall at the bus stop shelter. The children wanted to put toys and children's books at the bus stop, but Sua did not allow them because she feared they would miss the bus while playing with toys.

Sua, a mother of two, now knows how to persuade her children. Sua's motherhood, which, despite her children's persistence, eventually persuades them to respectfully obey her mother, and quietly understands her own thoughts, was something I envy so much.

When Sua was breastfeeding her two children, I was so envious of Sua holding her baby in her arms. Although the children are now developing their own thoughts that are different from their mother's, it was so lovely to see the children who eventually became one with their mother in the family. Looking at the mother and children like that, I fell into a desperate feeling that I don't have, and the chances are getting slimmer.

A yellow bus was coming. Ian first ran shouting, 'It's the bus, Rachel!', Rachel followed her brother.

The two children took turns in my arms before boarding, got on the bus, sat on their seats, and waved again to go to school. How adorable are these children?

When the children return home from school, Brian will be waiting for the school bus, just like his father who worked at the winery and always waited to meet Brian and me.

Time will pass like that, and the beautiful way of life will naturally flow over time and form generations.

After sending the children on the school bus, I was walking very slowly home. The cold wind over Lake Ontario blew through my armpits and down the nape of my neck, so I wrapped the hem of my scarf around my neck once more. As I wrapped the thick hem around my neck, I suddenly remembered Michael, who came to my house without a call the day I opened the parking lot door to go to the library. Late summer and autumn passed and we didn't talk to each other until winter, and when Michael came to me without a phone call, it must have been an urgent matter, and he seemed to be delivering an envelope to me. I accidentally went home with Michael and got the envelope Michael had given me, but as I was afraid to open it, I left it on the table in my room.

When Michael asked, 'I want to hear your thoughts, when can you tell me?' I said, 'It won't be long'. But now I thought I should look at the envelope.

After all, that was the promise. Time to rethink our relationship. If either one of the two doesn't want to continue the relationship, it stops. So, it was a promise between Michael's future and mine, and during that time, the two intentionally did not communicate with each other.

How carefully did he come to that conclusion? Since I was silent, he must have taken the first step because he couldn't stand his impatience. That was the conclusion I reached, so I already knew the meaning of the envelope.

A strong thought that I must no longer avoid it arose in my head as I wandered through the white snow. I told him that it wouldn't take long, so Michael would be waiting for the news, and since Michael was patient enough to put up with his temper, I had to come to a conclusion without any regrets. If I should sign something, I have to sign it and I have to clear the memories that remain in my heart.

If we add up the nine years we've been married, and the long time since we were younger, Michael and I have had a pretty persistent relationship, and now it's going to end in a bad relationship. There seemed to be no such thing as a bad relationship. Because those hours of the nine years also diluted the time of the nightmares that were younger.

I walked slowly and did not enter the house right away, but stood for a moment in the back yard behind the house overlooking Lake Ontario. Water chased by the wind was foaming and rushing in. The old oak tree had all its leaves blown away by the wind, and the tree house in its arms was curled up in a deep hibernation.

'Why are you standing like that when it's cold, Anna?'

Instead of a tree house, an oak tree seemed to be talking to me. The oak tree that has been watching me since I was seven years old was a tree that knew me.

'Because I have a hard time.'

I looked up at the oak tree and said to myself, as it was so hard, I was afraid that I would break down, so I wanted to clear my mind while being hit by a sharp wind. It was to take care of me. If there was even a single trace of regret, I had to cut it off first with the determination of the wind.

The oak tree said to me. 'Sometimes I get sick too. When I was sick, I thought of the time when you rode up and down my back and laughed. When I looked back at my old age, everything that had approached me had passed. Anything that bothers you now will pass.'

These words that an oak tree would tell me were somehow like the words my real mother would tell me if she were alive.

'Mom!'

I looked at Lake Ontario, Lake Titicaca in my heart, and called my mother in the language of my childhood. When I called my real mother, Quechuao, like a foreign language that I did not know, it just burst out of me.

Although the ground was covered with snow to the point the ankles, the lake with the gloomy winter sky was never swayed by the snow.

I wanted to be an oak tree that was enduring a windswept wind, I also wanted to be a winter lake that embraced the snow falling into its heart. I wanted to take my misfortune without being swayed by it no matter what tremendous thing happens in front of me. I wanted to embrace it as a precious part of my life. Just as I am now calm, even though I buried my first love deep in my heart, I wanted to bury the time I had with Michael.

'Hold me, Mom.'

But I, who could never become a winter lake by myself, was clinging to my mother again. Looking back, it seemed that I had first found my mother, who was faint in my memory whenever I felt desperate. She was a Peruvian mother, out of this world, not Joanne's mother.

'I want to have a good time. I don't want to get sick either, Mom.'

The cold wind bothered my eyes. Tears kept flowing from my eyes. Life has passed, and so has Michael.

That's how I send them all. I just wanted to let him go calmly, so that when we met one day on the street, I could say ‘How are you, Michael?’. I wanted to break up like that.

Although I did not hear any answer from my mother, I was able to calm my heart by looking at the lake and oak trees that held my eyes and knew how to blow away even a gust of wind, so I came back to my mother's house. And I first found a pen and put it on the table. It was because of my heart, not knowing when it might collapse again if I don't hurry.

I untied my scarf, took off my coat, and sat down on the chair. Then I opened the envelope, the envelope that had been lying on the table for a long time. I took a deep breath and pretended to be calm, but my fingers were trembling.

Inside the envelope were several documents folded in four folds. I thought of it as a document for divorce in this country. I opened the papers. I'd rather be quiet now.

‘...?’

Thinking that this could not be the case, I pulled out the documents from the envelope and checked the front and the back.

‘...!’

No matter how much I looked, it wasn't a document that required my sign. It was an e-flight reservation ticket in my name and Michael's, printed in Toronto - Lima, Lima - Cusco.

‘Cuzco? That Inca Cusco?’

In my quiet bewildered mind, the word Cusco, along with the word Inca, came to mind. It was Cusco, the capital of the Inca, to meet the legendary bird condor.

‘O Almighty Condor, wait for me in the Inca Square of Cusco’

It was a part of the lyrics of 'El Condor Pasa'.

‘That Cusco?’

It was as if Michael suddenly poured a bubble-causing soft drink into my bewildered mind while pretending to be calm. It felt like my brain was swelling with air bubbles. Now, the thought that everything would be over with just one sign suddenly got entangled with air bubbles and got lost in direction.

“Michael!”

The image of him swinging me like this and smiling with his heart

passed by.
It was an absurd reversal.
"Michael!"
Looking back, I was swayed by my emotions. Before being swayed, I had to rule and calm myself, but I was the reed of Lake Titicaca. I should have suppressed the indignant imagination that paralyzed my reason and provoked only my emotions to anger, but I rather encouraged it and was swayed by it. It was a time when rational judgment was more important than ever, and it took a long time for it, and it was a matter for the rest of the lives of the two of them, and I was finally trying to settle a relationship with the future at stake. So the grudge Brian had towards his mother, the grudge that I wanted to imitate, I was pouring out on Michael at this important moment.
'How did he know that I wanted to go to the land of the Inca?'
The country I've never been to since I left when I was seven, it was my land, but it was my hometown and my past that I didn't want to reveal to Michael. Recalling the time when I was so much teased for being different from others was not a pleasant thing for each other.
By the way, I was planning to go with my mother, but for some reason, not with my mother, but with Michael?
Had I not known my husband, Michael so much? Did I say I forgot, but I couldn't forget everything and lived for nine years, engulfed in the memories of my childhood? Or is there some other meaning I haven't figured out yet?
With the e-ticket, I was thrown into tens of thousands of thoughts.

At this point, I felt like I had to stop the time of deep misunderstanding about relationships.
If each other needed a long period of silence, now it seemed like it would be the order of time to break the silence and share each other's thoughts through conversation. And I wanted to know the true meaning of the ticket.
I called Michael.
"Anna!"
Michael's voice took my breath away. I took a deep breath not to hear my mind.
"I missed you, Anna!"
He didn't even give me time to call his name.
"Don't tell me, 'wait longer!' I can't do it anymore!"

He was grumpy while whining. He was a cute boy. Looking back, there were times when he seemed like a cute boy. So I hugged him and put my lips on his forehead. And because that was what called his first kiss and that innocence attracted me more.

"Let me talk too, Michael!"

As if stroking a mischievous son, I smiled.

"Wow, now you are my wife!"

Michael's voice sounded like it was flying with soap bubbles.

We decided to meet at his restaurant.

24. Shall We Dance

Michael was waiting for me at the entrance of the restaurant.
"Anna!"
As soon as I got out of the car, he hugged me, looked into my face, and kissed me happily. He seemed to have forgotten all of his modest behavior. Now he was my husband, Michael, whom I knew. It was as if we were in a devotee as the cold energy that stood between them disappeared.
The restaurant that Michael started with a winery he inherited from his father was a business he devoted his passion and affection into. However, Michael and I did not eat at the restaurant except for special occasions. Michael liked the food I made, and most of all, because I didn't want my family members to visit Michael's restaurant often.
As Michael escorted me in, the waiter took my coat.
The restaurant was quiet even though it was dinner time. The lights were soft and the music was quiet. I thought music was familiar to my ears. It was a 'lonely shepherd'.
'Michael, you!'
I smiled. It was like Michael prepared music for me.
"Are you running your business right?"
I looked around, but no one was.
"No, I think it will close soon."
For a business owner who is going to close soon, he was overjoyed.
A candle in a glass bowl was shyly burning on the table.
I looked around again. It kept bothering me that the music was quiet and no customers came in.
"Is this restaurant so quiet every day?"
It seemed to be about to close the door after starting ambitious. Was our business not going smoothly because our family was not

comfortable? The ripple effect of the uneasy relationship between Michael and me seemed bigger than I expected, and I was sorry that my stubbornness and negligence played a part in his business.

"You didn't see the notice I had put up as you came in. Tonight, it was announced that we could not accommodate guests due to circumstances."

"Because of me?"

"No, because of you and me."

Michael laughed playfully.

"The guests who made a reservation, we agreed to serve them the other day and asked for their understanding."

Michael said cheerfully.

It was then that I looked closely at Michael. There was confidence and leisure on his face to enjoy his own job.

"It's really going to close."

While I was joking, the waiter came with a bottle of wine. I thought he was drinking.

Waiter filled my glass first, then Michael's.

"It's non-alcoholic wine. It's ours."

"Are you now?"

"I don't drink wine."

Michael said with a determined look.

'How can I drink again?'

"Right. It wouldn't have been easy."

"It was easier than being without you."

I didn't know right away if Michael was joking again or if he was serious.

"Michael, you're a person who really makes up your mind!"

I complimented him a little.

"Yeah, except for one thing."

Then the waiter brought the food and Michael and I started eating.

"How did you know that I wanted to go to Peru?"

In fact, this was something Michael didn't know. Only my mother knew that I always had my hometown in my heart. The fact that every time I played the zamponya, I missed my hometown. So my mother would have said, 'Anna, you and I, let's go to Peru.'

"I didn't know you wanted to go home. I never asked and you never told me. Actually, I talked to your mother on the phone a lot."

He said something unexpected. I knew that my mother had a great antipathy for Michael since I went through it, but she called him frequently, and moreover, my mother never said a word to me.

"I couldn't contact you, so I had to ask your mother how you were, if Anna was eating well and was not ill, every day."

'Everyday?'

"Yes. you didn't tell me not to talk to your mother, did you?"

Michael's expression was natural.

'So every day without me knowing?'

It would not have been possible without the conspiracy of the two of them. Even if Michael had been hiding, my mother would have given me any hints, but she was hiding it too.

"At the same time, I learned about your mother's memory symptoms, and later, I was curious about how your mother was doing. I'm not a doctor, but I thought it would be good for your mother to keep looking back and holding on to the bad memories. And I heard a lot about you. Stories that I didn't know even though I had lived with you for nine years, stories I didn't want to know, and stories that you probably wouldn't even think to tell me. Then I found out that your mother wanted to go to Peru with you."

It was because I had cut contact with Michael anyway, but I was more surprised than sad that my mother, who met me every day in the same house, drinking tea and talking, kept the whole process a secret.

How much time had we spent sitting at the table together, drinking tea together, playing games and talking together, but I was so confused that my mother was keeping her mouth shut so that she wouldn't even make a mistake. I couldn't help but get confused between the two facts that my mother's memory might be really bad, or maybe it wasn't a problem at all.

"One day, your mother said, 'Michael, can you go to Peru with Anna, I think it would be too much for me on a long trip.'

So I asked, 'Mother, do you believe me?'

Michael also knew that my mother had bad feelings for him.

At that time, when I had to go my mother's home from the hospital after a miscarriage, Michael seemed to remember that my mother cut off his offer and took me to her house by force. It was then that I also felt that my mother distrusted Michael.

"Your mother was very honest. She said, 'There was no other way at this point, Michael. I'm going to try to trust you,' That was what your mother said."

Those words actually made him feel that my mother already believed in him, Michael said.

"I'm sorry, Anna. It would have been better if that was my idea. From now on, I will try harder to get to know you. Because I didn't know you all, I was drunk and talked to you, and I used my power to make you suffer, and in the end I even let my baby go... Those two red lines seemed to rebuke me."

Michael brought up the past that he had been trying to hide.

"Then why didn't you say anything if you could blame me? I was really scared back then."

In fact, I couldn't repeat myself to someone who had already remembered every single act of drunkenness because of the two red lines. Just thinking about painful things and looking back on them will be a punishment.

"I didn't know you all, but you all knew me. Without you I couldn't be."

Michael grabbed my hand on the table.

'Do I know all Michael?'

I could never say I knew everything. I didn't even know that Michael was like this at this moment. I didn't know that Michael spoke to my mother every day to get to know me better, I didn't know that the two red lines were scolding him, and I didn't know that he was afraid of me.

"Why didn't you tell me before booking the ticket?"

"If I had said it, you would have said 'no!'Your mother said, in fact, while Anna was growing up, when she had to say 'No!', she couldn't say 'No!'So, even if Anna says 'No!'this time, you shouldn't listen to it as the truth. I'm sure Anna would want to say 'yes!' Even though your mother told me that, I was still afraid of your 'No!'"

'Oh, mother!'

My mother already knew my habit of answering when I was a child. The fact that I always changed the answer, which Brian was able to say without hesitation, 'no!'to 'yes!'. The fact that it was the part between my mother and me that I couldn't overcome.

"Can I understand your answer as 'yes?'"

I smiled and nodded. Michael tightened my grip again, saying, 'Thank you, Anna.'

"And I have something to tell you. The trip to Peru was your mother's idea, but what I say now is my opinion. So we had to meet."

Michael talked a lot today. Michael cleared his mind for a moment.

"Anna, what do you think about adoption?"

"Adoption?"

It was so unexpected that I sat down and looked into Michael's eyes.

"Yes, adoption. You will be a good mother, and I think I can be a good father too."

Michael's eyes were serious and his voice calm.

"Your mother and father did it too."

Michael's words were so sudden and shocking that I didn't know what to say first.

"This is what I was thinking the whole time I started living apart from you. I have inquired about the adoption process through various agencies, but what was more important was your opinion, so I have been waiting for this day."

'That was why you asked me to give you my answer quickly.'

That was the reason for the utter misunderstanding I had.

"Michael, do you like babies?"

I already knew how long he waited for the baby.

"Yeah, I didn't say it because I was afraid it would burden you, but I waited a long time. That's why I was reluctant to meet friends."

'Yeah, that's when you started getting your hands on alcohol again and starting to get rough.'

"Michael, growing up was not easy."

I said a little coldly. It wasn't something that started as a temporary feeling anyway.

"Michael, I grew up in a good environment, but inside me there was a pain that even my parents didn't know about. That pain made me a child who had to say 'yes' to what I wanted to say 'no'.

It made me a child afraid of change.

That pain made me into a child who was always passive in the things I wanted to do, a child with limitations in myself. This was a problem I had to overcome on my own, and it had a huge impact on the formation of my personality, but I couldn't get rid of my pain as easily as a deeply ingrained habit."

"I grew up in a good environment like you, Anna. But I always had trouble even when everything was affluent, and I shattered my parents' hopes. I want to raise our child with you. Children grew up watching their parents. So I thought of adopting. I want to meet the baby there with you."

"Michael!"

Michael was talking about the child now. Is this my husband Michael who frustrated me and made me rethink my relationship for a long time?

"There? In Cusco?"

Michael nodded his head.

"Oh, Michael, you surprised me many times today!"

How did he come to think of the long-awaited life in the land of the Inca? I looked at Michael.

"Do you think we can be good parents?"

I said looking at Michael.

"Of course, you and I will be good parents together."

"Okay!"

I felt a certain energy rising out of control in my heart, which seemed to be about to collapse after losing hope of conception. The baby to be held in my arms will be both thrilling and joyous. It was also the conviction of the relationship that existed between Michael and me.

"If someone bothers my child like the naughty Michael when he was young, then I'll come out, just like Brian did."

Michael chuckled.

"You thought more than me, thank you, thank you so much for thinking more than me."

This time I took Michael's hand. Actually, I wanted to hug Michael.

"Do you want to hug me?"

Michael frowned and joked. He probably remembered the words what I had said when Michael revealed himself about alcoholism in his car on the Parkway before we got married. It was the day of our first kiss. I said 'yes' and smiled.

It was then that Michael gestured to the waiter who had been standing far away. The music, which seemed to have subsided, changed in an instant to another song, overwhelming the large restaurant in an instant. It was like a fountain rising into the air with great momentum.

'El Condor Pasa!'

It was not a lonely sobbing spit out like a sigh, but a sound of impulse that made me want to surrender to the rhythm in Michael's arms, and it was a sensual melody that loosened the knots of tension that were tying my body. And it was the saxophone's cry to become one with the sound within it as the sound leads. I wanted to untie all the knots of tension that were tying me.
It was then that Michael got up from his seat. He came up to me from the other side and put out a hand politely towards me.

"Shall we dance Mrs. Anna Evans?"

He was staring down at me and I was barely holding back something that was boiling in my head until it finally exploded, so I accidentally put my hand on his hand. He snatched me up and put me in front of him. Then he put one arm around my waist, took my hand with the other, and left us to the melody of the saxophone.

"How long have we been dancing like this, Anna?"

Michael's voice as he stepped on the steps was a whisper in my ear. I knew it wasn't meant to be dancing after a while, but meant to say, "How long has it been since we've been holding each other?"

"It feels like ten years have passed."

How could I have passed the day and the seasons without being hugged like this, I thought.

"I hate being alone, I will never be alone again."

Michael grumbled like a child. We moved from table to table to the music, talking softly. Tonight was a day when there should be no guests.

"Neither do I, never again."

Then I buried my face in his chest. His heartbeat entered my ears.
Michael grabbed my waist with both arms. My arms were wrapped around his neck in between.

"El Condor Pasa"

A sad song, I didn't know that this song, which always sang tears, would make us dance. Tears became dances with Michael.

"Oh, isn't that a dream, Anna?"

I replied 'No' in his arms.

"Anna, I didn't know you liked 'El Condor Pasa,'and I didn't know how desperately you wanted to go home. Did I ever know anything about you?"

As he hugged me and danced, Michael continued talking. It must have been something I had never done before and wanted to say.

"What's the only thing you can't do though you make up your mind, Michael?"

It was a question that reminded him of his words, 'Except for one thing.'

"Oh, that, breaking up with you. So I was so scared."

"I was scared too, Michael. I couldn't even open the envelope you gave me."

I whispered silently.

"I'm afraid you'll never see me again..."

Then he buried his face in the nape of my neck. With his face buried, Michael said nothing for a moment. As I moved to the music, I could sense the slight tremor on the nape of my neck.

"I can't do it without you, but you..."

Then he stopped talking again.

"Oh, Michael!"

Michael's arms wrapped around my waist and wrapped around my shoulders, and my hands wrapped around his face. Now the melody of the saxophone soared into the air and screamed, and finally, it was two streams of fountains that wrapped around each other and wet each other.

"I was so afraid, too, that I might never see you again."

I found his lips as I stroked his wet face in my wrapped hands.

We both looked at each other with wet cheeks and wet lips feeling each other and writhing wet.

We didn't care if the waiters were watching, because we were a couple who didn't meet even though we were close to each other, so that would make sense.

And now we are dancing the reunion dance.

25. Meet the Condor

Finally, Michael and I boarded the plane. It was a flight to Peru.
How long has it been?
I am going with my husband to the homeland I left when I was seven years old. It was a trip I decided to go with my mother.
What my mother's saying that she wanted to go to Peru with me was a plan to let me and Michael go? If so, my mother's plan has been perfected.

'Your mom has privacy too, Anna.'
When I asked my mother, 'Mother, you talked to Michael every day, and didn't say a word to me,' she smirked.
'I could have blinded you, but I failed with your father. You know, your father asked, 'Are you dating these days?'
My mother laughed again, saying that father was jealous of her even though he knew it was Michael. It was the first cheerful laugh, just like when my mother was in good health since her memory was confused.
'Anna, actually, my mouth wanted to talk, so it was hard to put up with it. I should have known Michael. It was a major event that took my daughter's life at stake.'
Could it not have been that the mother struggled every day, holding onto the memories that kept disappearing for the sake of her daughter's life?
Oh my mother! Ms. Joanne Hills had me confused again. It was because my mother was too smart and planned for dementia. I decided not to believe my mother's illness. I decided to trust only my loving mother.
Now Michael and I are going to Peru. What does that place look like? A place where my real mother died giving birth to my younger brother, and there was neither my father nor my brother Mario. I have no idea

what awaits me and what I remember still remains. The place where Lake Titicaca was and the reeds were thick, the place where people suffered from the hot sun and harsh winds lived a long life. Is the place still the same as the one I left there? Even the smallest part of what I knew about that vast land, my country with the Inca ruins, was almost gone from my memory and faded. But the vitality of the faint is persistent, and I have never forgotten that I am the daughter of Peru.

'Almighty Condor, wait for me in the Inca Square of Cusco'

Looking at Lake Ontario like Lake Titicaca from the tree house, how many days I sang, how many days I missed the land with a melody.
I am going with my husband Michael towards the Cusco square.
The condor that will wait for us there, the name of freedom that is not bound by anything, is it really in the shape of a big bird? Peruvian father said that the condor was a legendary immortal bird.
The legendary bird waiting for Michael and me in Cusco seems to be in the form of a baby waiting for Michael and me.
'How could you come up with such a grand idea? The joy that my Anna, whom I bore with my heart, gave me was always undeserved. My daughter and her son-in-law are sure to be good parents.'
These were the words of my mother, who knew Michael and my decision.
As my mother said, I am going to meet the baby that Michael and I will make a heartfelt resolution every day to become good parents, the baby who will make Michael and me good mother and father, and the baby that Michael and I will bear with our hearts. The daughter of Peru, who had only a faint memory, had another Peru, and as my real father said, the condor must be an immortal bird.
Finally, the plane, which had been rolling slowly, accelerated with a loud roar. At the point where it could no longer roll, the plane finally kicked off the ground and began to soar into the sky.
I grabbed Michael's hand tightly. I am going with El Michael to the place I left with my mothcr, fathcr, and young Brian.
The child I met in an unfamiliar land, the child that bothered me the most, grew up to be a husband and went through a severe crisis.
"I want to hug my baby."
"Me too."
I said, leaning on Michael's shoulder.

The baby we will meet is an immortal bird, a Condor to be reborn in the arms of Michael and me.

The End.

El Condor

Author: Owe Sook Kim

Publishing House: Amazon Kindle
Publishing Date: 08-01- 2022

Owe Sook Kim
jean53@hanmail.net

Acknowledgement

Living in America, Anna called her Father once in a while to see how he was doing.

"I can't believe you've aged this much already... Don't die, Father."
Anna always ended her calls in tears saying, "Father, don't die."

Anna's father, Reverend James Hills said, "Anna always tells me not to die."

Always worried about her Father's age, Anna passed away first from heart attack. She was sixty years old.
Getting weaker from his old age, Reverend James Hills said crying, "Our Anna, always telling me not to die, went first..."

Anna was adopted from Costa Rica at the age of seven, long before I married Reverend James Hills. A family of three sons and one daughter became three sons and two daughters in Reverend James Hills' household.

I had never experienced adoption nor had anyone around me, so to see him adopt another daughter while raising four children, told me Reverend James Hills was no ordinary man. In truth, the writer in me saw the source material when I looked at the adoption and **the warm** happy family. But I couldn't bring myself to write because this was my family's story.

However, when Anna left us several years ago at the young age of sixty, while worrying about her Father's health, I began to think that I wanted to bring Anna to life through my stories.

I thought long and hard how I could bring Anna to life and in November of 2019, I began to write my novel, 'El Condor'.
To name the main character Anna and have her be an adoptee was my way of confessing my feelings for Anna and my way of remembering

her.

The story of Anna being adopted by the Hills family, falling in love with Brian and leaving, then falling in love with Michael, getting married to almost getting divorced, and adopting a child from Peru, all this was from my imagination.

I became young Anna and when Anna was young, I grew up with Anna as she became older and fell in love. I experienced her love and her heartbreaks.
At the age of late sixties, I experienced love through the characters of my work and it will forever be with me.

I had a few things that I wanted to say with this work.
I wanted to show Anna's change from living in a poor family in Peru to being adopted to a Canadian family and putting down her roots. I also wanted to show that the condor represents deep roots by having Anna adopt a child from Peru.
Most of all, I wanted to have Anna, who left us too early, come to life through my work and be loved and always be happy, overcoming hardships.

Anna Hills, the daughter of my husband Reverend James Hills, may have passed, but Anna Hills will be happy again forever reborn as Anna Evans in my work 'El Condor'.
From the start and to the end of the story, I became Anna and cried and loved. I was happy while writing because I loved her.

I hope the readers of 'El Condor' will be happy along with my Anna.

From Canada, Niagara On The Lake.

Oew Sook Kim

About The Author

Oew Sook Kim

Myongji College Creative Arts
1991 'Legacy' A short novel, 'Literature and Consciousness'

Published Works
Novels: 'Road Inside You', 'Ice Wine', 'Happy Wedding',
'Traces of Wind', 'That House, Nursing Home', 'El Condor'
Novella: 'Two Mountains', 'The Wind's Sleep', 'Magic'
Prose: 'Wind, Then Happiness', 'The Dancing Fork and Knife'

Awards
1998 Han Ha Eun Literary Award
2003 Korean Christain Literary Award
2006 Overseas Korean Literature Award

2007	Korean American Literary Award
2010	Cheongang Literary Award
2016	Jikji Literary Award
2018	Overseas Koran Novel Literary Award

*2005 Short Story 'Avalanche' voted into 'The Year's Examining Novels' collection

*Novels 'Happy Wedding', 'Traces of Wind', 'That House, Nursing Home' serialized in Canada Korea Times. 'El Condor' serialized in Canada Korea Times website.

Contact
jean53@hanmail.net

Printed in Great Britain
by Amazon